The Mentoris Project is a series of novels and biographies about the lives of great Italians and Italian-Americans: men and women who have changed history through their contributions as scientists, inventors, explorers, thinkers, and creators. The Barbera Foundation sponsors this series in the hope that, like a mentor, each book will inspire the reader to discover how she or he can make a positive contribution to society.

A NOVEL BASED ON THE LIFE OF
THOMAS AQUINAS

HUMBLE SERVANT OF TRUTH

Margaret O'Reilly

THE
MENTORIS
PROJECT

Barbera Foundation, Inc.
P.O. Box 1019
Temple City, CA 91780

More information at www.mentorisproject.org

ISBN: 978-1-947431-12-6

Library of Congress Control Number: 2018903998

All net proceeds from the sale of this book will be donated to Barbera Foundation, Inc. whose mission is to support educational initiatives that foster an appreciation of history and culture to encourage and inspire young people to create a stronger future.

Contents

Foreword

First and foremost, Mentor was a person. We tend to think of the word *mentor* as a noun (a mentor) or a verb (to mentor), but there is a very human dimension embedded in the term. Mentor appears in Homer's *Odyssey* as the old friend entrusted to care for Odysseus's household and his son Telemachus during the Trojan War. When years pass and Telemachus sets out to search for his missing father, the goddess Athena assumes the form of Mentor to accompany him. The human being welcomes a human form for counsel. From its very origins, becoming a mentor is a transcendent act; it carries with it something of the holy.

The Barbera Foundation's Mentoris Project sets out on an Athena-like mission: We hope the books that form this series will be an inspiration to all those who are seekers, to those of the twenty-first century who are on their own odysseys, trying to find enduring principles that will guide them to a spiritual home. The stories that comprise the series are all deeply human. These books dramatize the lives of great Italians and Italian-Americans whose stories bridge the ancient and the modern, taking many forms, just as Athena did, but always holding up a light for those living today.

Whether in novel form or traditional biography, these books plumb the individual characters of our heroes' journeys. The power of storytelling has always been to envelop the reader in a vivid and continuous dream, and to forge a link with the subject. Our goal is for that link to guide the reader home with a new inspiration.

What is a mentor? A guide, a moral compass, an inspiration. A friend who points you toward true north. We hope that the Mentoris Project will become that friend, and it will help us all transcend our daily lives with something that can only be called holy.

—Robert J. Barbera, President, Barbera Foundation
—Ken LaZebnik, Editor, The Mentoris Project

Chapter One

THE FIRE OF FAITH

The sun was a symbol of glory and splendor in medieval heraldry, signifying nobility deserving of the highest honor. The radiance it implied was nowhere brighter than in the heart and mind of Thomas Aquinas, a medieval philosopher, theologian, and much more. He was a humble servant of truth with a generous spirit, and above all, he was a lover of the Author of Truth. Imposing in appearance but gentle in mien, Thomas is often depicted in paintings with a sun over his heart. The beams of light that emanate from that sun radiate beyond the canvas and across time to the present age, illuminating the minds of men to "fire their hearts," according to Pope Pius XI in his *Studiorum Duce*. His ardor for truth centuries ago fanned the flame of reason like a bellows in the fire of faith from that time on. The flame still burns today, sometimes dimly, sometimes intensely bright.

Thomas of Aquino was born into a life of privilege and promise in the heart of medieval Italy in 1225. His home was a castle built for the protection of the renowned Monte Cassino, a Benedictine monastery just northeast of Naples. His family was connected with much of the nobility that dominated thirteenth-century Europe. He was poised for a life of privilege and achievement.

Ironically, Thomas himself wanted nothing more than quiet simplicity and detachment. He longed to devote himself to learning and teaching others to see what he himself saw with almost supernatural clarity. His mind was his true gift, and like the genius of Mozart, of Shakespeare, or of Michelangelo, it was not meant to be enjoyed alone, but to change the world.

Recognizing the greatness of the created world, Thomas sought to plumb its depths and scan its heights, leaving no room for darkness, doubt, or obscurity. He grappled with a myriad of questions and contemplated profound concepts; no problem was ignored or treated lightly if its solution lay within his power. For the sake of knowledge, for the love of something greater than himself, he labored tirelessly with his mind.

Thomas Aquinas was a medieval man, but also a model for our times and, in fact, for all time. He loved truth, and through the use of reason he sought to illuminate it for all to see. He had no fear of what reason might discover because he firmly believed that all truth is united, that there can be no real conflict between one truth and another. Science, philosophy, metaphysics, politics, and faith can coexist unabashedly. True freedom, he knew, lay in that conviction.

His contribution to humanity is great, and his reputation traditionally has been proportionate. Even now, no one can lightly disregard the thought of Thomas Aquinas, except perhaps out of ignorance. It is as valuable today as it has ever been to contemplate the unparalleled brilliance of his work and the genuine beauty of his life.

Chapter Two

O TEMPORA

As the first light of dawn crept over the slopes of Monte Asprano and into the historic Valle di Comino, a hermit's lonely footfall could be heard along the rocky pathway outside Roccasecca. Visitors were not uncommon at this fortified "dry rock" atop the rolling Southern Italian hillside. Since antiquity it had been a convenient way station for invading armies and a strategic gateway to the broad valley below, the site of ancient battles. Even now, strangers came and went on imperial business, church concerns, and mundane family matters without arousing much curiosity. But the unremarkable footsteps of the hermit on this otherwise-unremarkable morning bore a significance that would echo through time.

The pious hermit was known to the family d'Aquino, but rarely emerged from his hermitage deep in the cypress forest. Today, he came with a message for the lady of the castle atop the *rocca*, Countess Theodora. She was a formidable woman of the family of Lombard, a lineage that united her with some of the most powerful kingdoms of the medieval world. Her marriage to Landolfo d'Aquino further widened the sphere of her connections. Count d'Aquino's family was related through marriage to Frederick Barbarossa, whom Landolofo had served until the death of that Holy Roman Emperor in 1190. Now the flag of Aquino flew behind the banner of Barbarossa's grandson, Frederick II.

Frederick, a Hohenstaufen and a distant cousin of the Aquinos, was known to a wary Europe as the *stupor mundi*, the "Wonder of the World." He was a military genius with an insatiable appetite for power. By political maneuvering he would become king of Germany, Sicily, and Jerusalem, and Holy Roman Emperor. It was in Frederick's last role that Count Landolfo d'Aquino found himself bound to serve as knight and judge. Landolfo was an honorable man in his own right, a loyal Catholic, the lord of two castles, and father to nine children. His older sons, too, served in the ranks of the Holy Roman Emperor.

The hermit on the *rocca*, however, was not concerned with the lineage of the countess or of her husband. His message, received while deep in prayer, had to do with the baby she bore, her eighth child.

When she met him in the tapestry-lined vestibule he told her, "My Lady, I have a commission. Forgive me for intruding on you, but I feel compelled…"

"Certainly, Father. No need to apologize," she answered graciously.

"It will seem strange I am sure, however it must be said. I am but the messenger." The lady nodded. The hermit continued. "It has been revealed to me that your unborn son will one day enter the Order of Friars Preachers and so great will be his learning and sanctity that in his day no one will be found to equal him."

Lady Theodora was pleasant enough. She was not easily impressed and this prediction seemed highly improbable. She thanked the old man for his peculiar message, begged his prayers for her family, and bade him good day.

From behind her heavy brocade skirts, her small daughters, Adalasia and Mary, peered curiously at the lean, bald man as he gave his solemn blessing and went out. The countess shook her head. "What an extraordinary man. Serene and utterly unpretentious, but how preposterous!"

The girls were puzzled, "What did he say, Mother?" Adalasia asked. At five years of age, she was the elder of the two girls. "What does he mean?"

"Oh, nothing of importance…nothing at all likely," her mother replied.

Having delivered his prophecy, the hermit retreated, his duty fulfilled and his conscience set at ease. He had done what he somehow knew he had to do. It was a surprisingly precise prediction, with nothing ambiguous about it. Obviously the Aquinos were not unaccustomed to greatness; they were prominent figures in this region. They were not renowned for great holiness or scholarship, but if a child of theirs should show an inclination to the religious life, they would expect him to seek out a well-established and respected order, such as the nearby Benedictines. The newly formed and somewhat dubious Order of Friars Preachers, followers of Dominic de Guzman, was countercultural to these people of power and wealth. It would have been a scandal to allow any one of their children to join a group of homeless, begging priests.

In any case, the unfolding of events indicates that the hermit's message was not received with unmixed joy, or even with credence. Perhaps it was not given much serious thought at all. For the Aquino family, more pressing matters were at hand. Even as the sound of the hermit's footsteps receded, a thunderhead of discord and war, tyranny and destruction was gathering around them.

The castle at Roccasecca had been the stronghold of the counts of Aquino for most of three hundred years. Built by a Benedictine abbot in 994 as part of a much-needed outward defense for the Abbey of Monte Cassino, the castle fortress became home to the noble Aquino family four years later and eventually they were entrusted with the role of protector. Theodora and Landolfo themselves never lived in the town of Aquino, visible from their fortress turret. But because the castle and the town both lay within the county of Aquino, the family name had always been associated with that ancient town.

Over the years, members of their wider family had lived and held positions of influence there, mingling their name with its rich layers of history. The church that served the Aquinos' spiritual needs, *Santa Maria della Libera*, stood upon the ruins of an ancient temple of Hercules. Nearby could be seen a triumphal arch, built in the first century to honor Roman triumvir, Marc Antony. *Aquinum*, as it had been known to antiquity, was originally founded by the Volsci, an early Italic tribe once dominant in Southern Italy. Because it was situated along the inland route from Rome to Naples, Via Latina, the town had grown into a bustling municipality familiar to Cicero and Juvenal among other notable figures. Emperors, philosophers, and poets originated there, and although it was razed in the sixth century by invading Goths, it had revived and spread into the more fertile surrounding land.

For some time, Landolfo's extended family held title over the entire county of Aquino and later over Acerra as well. Landolfo's cousin, Thomas I, was Count of Acerra and viceroy of most of the southern Italian peninsula.

When the hermit paid his visit to the Aquinos at Roccasecca, the political climate of Italy was such as to drive all other concerns into the background, especially because the Aquino family was unfortunately very much in the foreground. Their castle was located near the disputed border of the papal territories, the *Patrimonium Sancti Petri*, and the kingdom known as the Two Sicilies. Under Emperor Frederick II Hohenstaufen, the Two Sicilies comprised an expanding empire that united the lower half of the Italian peninsula to the Island of Sicily. Although the emperor was a relative of the Aquinos, he seemed oblivious to all that did not pertain to his vision of world dominance. Constant strife marked this place and time. The local Abbey of Monte Cassino was unluckily situated within the imperial region, but as a Catholic institution it was necessarily under papal authority. The Aquinos were faithful Roman Catholics and sworn protectors of the abbey, yet also they were also subjects in the service of the now hostile Emperor.

Turmoil was not exclusive to the kingdom of the Two Sicilies in which the Aquinos lived. The year 1227 witnessed the passing of three champions: one for truth, Pope Honorius III, who insisted on the importance of educating his clergy; one for charity, the almost universally beloved Francis of Assisi; and one for worldly power, the founder of the Mongol empire and the terror of Asia, Genghis Khan. These men symbolized the threefold forces that agitated Italy, and in fact most of Europe and Asia at this time.

All three passed from history in the year 1227, but the pivot points that they represented, the intellectual, spiritual, and the political realms, continued to clash violently. This mighty tempest was felt everywhere, not least of all within the family of Aquino in their castle at Roccasecca. Ironically, the same family that had been given charge of the castle for the sake of defending Monte Cassino was not uncommonly under imperial orders to attack the abbey. Such were the turbulent times in which they lived.

In the year 1220, Frederick Hohenstaufen was crowned Holy Roman Emperor by Pope Honorius III after a monumental struggle between his and the papal powers. At first, he appeared to be a friend and ally of the Church—albeit a tenuous one—and protector of the papal territories in Northern Italy. But that alliance cooled very quickly as his relentless will to conquer led to the slaughter of thousands of innocent but inconvenient subjects.

He had seemed magnificent in his youth, inspiring the confidence of his countrymen. But under the abrasions of time and power, he matured into a heartless leader who treated his subjects as mere pawns. They seemed to exist solely for his advantage; if they did not serve, they did not live. As his reign expanded from Germany to larger regions in the Two Sicilies, fear began to grip the people of Europe. Eventually Frederick Hohenstaufen would march into Jerusalem and crown himself king. He reigned in the name of Germany, Sicily, Jerusalem, and the entire Holy Roman Empire; but his laws were formed and enforced primarily in the interests of Frederick Hohenstaufen.

To the anguish of his southeastern Italian subjects, he imported tens of thousands of Saracens to the region of Apulia. These relocated Saracens manned his armies and contributed the taxes needed to sustain his military campaigns. To ensure that there would be little resistance to his Muslim colonies, Frederick ordered the massacre of the native Christian population in the vicinity, condoning the torture and execution of the priests and any other religious leaders there.

At about that time, Honorius III passed on to his eternal reward and Pope Gregory IX took the helm, prepared for battle. On account of Frederick's brutality and his thinly veiled disdain for the ecclesial authority that crowned him, Frederick found himself excommunicated from the Catholic Church by the solemn decree of Pope Gregory IX in that same momentous year of 1227.

Into this climate of political hostility, Theodora brought forth her newest son and at their church, the *Santuario de Santa Maria della Libera*, she had him baptized.

"His name will be Tommaso," the count announced to Friar Sandro, who was to baptize the boy that day.

"Ah, the Doubter is his patron, then," the priest smiled. "The holy apostle whose faith was tested and proved by his life and by his holy death. A fine name."

"It is a family name, as well, Father. It has served many men in my family with dignity. Think you not my cousin, the Count of Acerra, bears it well?"

"Indeed, a fine man, and a fine name," the amenable Friar Sandro agreed.

Under the lofty ceiling of the *Santuario* embellished with white-and-gold images of saints and angels, the infant squirmed in his mother's arms as the priest poured Holy Water over his head and pronounced the words of baptism. The child was called Thomas, a name that literally means "twin" and was associated with *San Tommaso Apostolo*, the "Doubter" of the Christian Gospels. But flowing through the veins of this infant was the antithesis of doubt. It was soon quite clear that he was endowed with a double portion of the spirit of truth.

About three years after Thomas' entry into the world, a violent thunderstorm descended on the *rocca* one night, as if to punctuate the political chaos that surrounded the Aquinos. Flashes of light flooded the nursery, illuminating its gray interior with an unearthly blue. The sound of thunder crashed like a battering ram shaking the castle walls. To young Thomas, it seemed as if the whole of nature were forcing itself into his room, and it was very angry. Placing a sturdy protective arm around his newest sister, known to the family as *bella neonata*, beautiful baby girl, he wriggled closer to their nurse and drifted off into an uneasy sleep. Sometimes he would jerk suddenly, or cry out in his sleep. Every thunderclap seemed to jar him into somnolent terror. Finally, the storm subsided and his sleep grew more profound. All the while, his baby sister lay quietly next to him. When he awoke, he found her soft, bald head beside him and gave it an affectionate kiss, gently, so as not to disturb her rest.

"What has happened?" Gaita, his nurse, who was usually so sure and calm, looked gray, and her voice shook. She stared at the motionless infant in the bed beside Thomas. He looked, too, and realized all at once that the little one had not moved in ever so long. Her dimpled arms were still, her head had been cold to his lips. "What has happened?" Gaita now fairly screamed.

Thomas' fearful wide brown eyes met the grief-stricken eyes of his nurse and he knew that something terrible had happened. In her distress she ushered Thomas abruptly from the room, calling over his head in anguished tones for help. His mother rushed in and Thomas was forgotten in the agony that followed.

Thomas and his four older sisters moved about the castle grounds warily that day, not daring or even wanting to break the silence that hung like a shroud. People came and went; his older brothers were sent for, but no one seemed to take notice of the younger children. Finally, their nurse called them to her and explained with a quavering voice that their *bella neonata* had been taken back to God. Lightning from the fearful storm had reached into the trundle during the night and struck her dead as she lay nestled beside her brother.

During the indistinct days that followed, her tiny coffin was dropped into the cold earth, Mass was offered, more people visited and left. While his mother grieved, a tonelessness filled the home of the noble Aquinos. Thomas watched silently and alone at night he wept.

Time kindly wove a web over his wounds, and the searing pain subsided, but the memory of Bella left a scar tender to the touch that not even the passage of years could erase.

"What is God?" Thomas wanted to know. He was now no longer a frightened toddler but a strapping little boy of five. He was forever asking that question, and he really wanted an answer. His pragmatic older brothers, Aimo, Landolfo, and Rinaldo, laughed at his questions, and his sisters, who were closer to him in age, would sometimes offer suggestions. "That's who made you, Tommaso," his biggest sister, Marrota, had said confidently. "God made everything in the world."

Theodora, who was not as old as Marrota but who was never wrong as far as he could tell, had often told him that God was in the church and that was why they had to be respectful and quiet there. He felt that all these things were true, but if God was in the church, and God made the world, what was He? None of their answers could fully satisfy the inquisitive young Aquino.

Father had told him that his Uncle Sinibaldi, the abbot of Monte Cassino, would help him find an answer to that question and to many others if he were a good boy and studied hard. "It will not be long now, Tommaso, before you will leave the *rocca* and go to Monte Cassino to live and study with the learned Benedictine fathers."

With naive contentment, he remembered the day in July when his father told him that the Holy Roman Emperor and the Holy Father, Gregory IX, were friends once more. It had been a tumultuous decade since Frederick was given the crown by Pope Honorius III. At that time, the proud emperor had vowed to lead a crusade to the Holy Land within two years, to reclaim for all of Christianity the land where Jesus himself had walked, taught, and died. He reneged on that promise repeatedly and instead invaded papal territories, killing the guiltless inhabitants and physically detaining Church officials from their attempts to convene for ecclesial business. As a result of his many transgressions, the newly elected Pope Gregory IX had issued a decree of excommunication against the emperor.

A few years earlier, Frederick had tried to pacify the Holy Father by finally setting sail for the Holy Land, although his allies at home continued to raid and pillage the papal lands. Gregory was not so easily manipulated. He reissued the ban against Frederick, and made it clear that none of the emperor's subjects were bound in conscience to serve the emperor so long as he persisted in his defiance. At last, the emperor seemed to relent, and now in nearby Cassino, the two men had reached an agreement of peace that they called the Treaty of San Germano. The following month, Gregory lifted the ban of excommunication against Frederick II.

Landolfo d'Aquino and his sons were relieved to be able to serve the Holy Roman Emperor in good conscience as their station required, while remaining faithful to the Holy Father. "The shadows have parted, boys," his father said that day, slapping Aimo on his broad shoulders. "The sun is shining on the Aquinos once more." Aimo smiled, genuinely relieved; he, more than any of the other boys, had been troubled by the conflict between their king to whom they owed allegiance, and their pope, the vicar of Christ on earth.

"But can it last, Father?" Landolfo wondered aloud. This was the second son of the count and his namesake. He and Rinaldo, inseparable for as long as Thomas could remember, were less sensitive to the moral quandary than Aimo, but not less interested in the practical ramifications of the accord.

"Who can say, son, these are uncertain times. We can but do our part one day at a time … and pray for the wit to avoid the disfavor of our two lords."

The competing claims upon the Aquinos had made their existence treacherous in recent years. Here was a respite at last. For Thomas, this friendship between the two powers meant that now he could stay with his uncle abbot at Monte Cassino and commence his education. His parents had arranged everything, entrusting the abbey with what seemed to him a wealth of gold for his support in the years to come.

It was May of 1231, almost a year after the treaty was signed and the ban lifted, when the day finally arrived for Thomas to begin his studies. His big brothers were rarely at the castle any more, occupied with their duties as *miles* for the king. Tommaso was his father's only "Little Man" about the place, and his mother's youngest child. He was plainly doted on, if not exactly spoiled; he loved his home on the *rocca*. He now realized that he would be leaving behind his sisters, Marrota, Theodora, Adalasia, and Mary. It was difficult to imagine a life without them or his mother and father. They would be only a few miles away, he knew, and could visit often. And they would still spend holidays together in the mountains. But it seemed a little hard.

"Come along," clucked Gaita as she took the now-somewhat-reluctant Thomas by the hand and led him down the rocky pathway. Mazzeo, the Aquinos' steward, had gone ahead to tend to final preparations for Thomas' entrance into Monte Cassino. The boy's possessions were few and barely filled the leather saddlebags on the steward's horse.

Thomas was brave as he said good-bye to his family outside his handsome home on the *rocca*. He shed tears, to be sure, but he did not make a fuss; he would not distress his parents in that way. "Farewell, young man," his father said, bowing formally. "Mind your Uncle Sinibaldi!" His mother held him tight for a long moment with glistening eyes. Adalasia and Mary cried outright. Theodora seemed confident that all would be well, and Marrota assured him with forced cheerfulness that they would visit him soon.

He hoped so. He gritted his teeth and reminded himself that, as hard as it was, father and mother knew what was best for him. And anyway, he really did want to know, "What is God?"

At about the same time that Thomas began his life with the Benedictine monks, his eldest brother, Aimo, set sail for the Holy Land on an expedition commissioned by the Holy Roman Emperor, Frederick II. The eldest Aquino son and the youngest left Roccasecca almost simultaneously, one on an errand of war and the other in the pursuit of knowledge. Each was a noble endeavor that reflected honor on the family and, happily, each son was well suited to the role he assumed.

Aimo was a man of action. To serve under the Holy Roman Emperor in a crusade was indeed an honor, albeit an uncertain one in these times. Thomas was contemplative, with pious instincts and an appetite for learning. His may have seemed a more humble career than that of the elder brother, but because of the Aquino family's social position and lofty connections, his family had reason to hope that his path would eventually lead to the abbacy. From there the possibilities were favorable: bishop, or cardinal perhaps, or, who could say, maybe even pope. The previous century had seen the ascent of the brilliant Desiderius from Abbot of Monte Cassino to Pope Victor III. In medieval Italy, a capable abbot of such an illustrious monastery could wield a great deal of influence. It was, at the least, a creditable position, and it carried a real possibility of prominence.

For his part, Thomas was content with the quiet order of his new life. Within the mosaic walls of the abbey, encouraged by the holy monks and in the company of other boys like himself, he learned to read and write with facility, and he mastered Latin. He was exposed to the writings of the greatest authors known to the world at the time: Tertullian, Cyprian, Hilary of Poitiers (called the Hammer of the Arians), and of course, the prolific and influential Augustine of Hippo, fourth-century bishop, philosopher and theologian. He heard, read, and took to heart Sacred Scripture and the Rule of Saint Benedict. The monastic wisdom epitomized by the dictum, *Ora et labora* (pray and work), for which Saint Benedict is renowned, became his own. He studied it and lived it out day to day, to the degree befitting a child.

But his peaceful existence was disrupted by the news that Aimo had been taken prisoner in the far off Holy Land. "He is not, thankfully, in the merciless hands of the Saracens there, whom the emperor has allegedly set out to defeat," his Uncle Abbot Sinibaldi told him, placing a comforting hand on his shoulder. "He is a hostage of Henry I, the rightful king of Cyprus."

"Why? What does Aimo have to do with the King of Cyprus?" Thomas asked. He looked up at his uncle searchingly. Thomas was tall for his age; his uncle was taller still. Yet both figures standing on the cobbled courtyard were dwarfed by the white façade of the abbey cathedral. As simply as he could, the abbot explained to his young charge that King Henry I was merely protecting his own homeland from the greed of Frederick Hohenstaufen, who wanted Cyprus for himself. Frederick had sent his hapless soldiers, Aimo among them, to the Eastern Mediterranean island of Cyprus to "govern" it, and to make a show of power in the Middle East, especially to Jerusalem.

"How unreliable are the promises of kings," Thomas shook his head, remembering the Treaty of San Germano, "when they can cause the fortunes of so many other people to change direction like the wind, simply because of their greed. Father was right when he said nothing is certain. Only God is sure."

The abbot agreed with his nephew's unexpected observation. Commiserating, he went on with his account. "The reports that have reached us here indicate that throughout the Kingdom of Jerusalem the Holy Roman Emperor has been fomenting dissension between the papal supporters and the imperial factions. His goal on undertaking this crusade is now plain. It is not to reclaim the Holy Land for Christianity as he pretended; it is, and always was, to claim that Kingdom for himself. He was successful in the mainland portion of the Kingdom, where he has seized the crown and declared himself king. But on the island of Cyprus, where Aimo had been sent, his forces were soundly repulsed."

Thomas listened in silence as his uncle continued.

"There, Frederick's troop of two thousand horsemen was defeated by a contingent of determined Cypriots about three hundred strong; sixty men were killed, and forty men were captured. Our Aimo was among the captives."

For as long as Thomas could remember, his eldest brother had been to him an example of gentleness and bravery. It was some comfort that his uncle seemed to think there was hope. He began at once to pray for Aimo's release. His father and mother, the abbot told him, were on their way to Rome to appeal directly to Pope Gregory on Aimo's behalf.

It was not long before the Holy Father intervened and arranged the ransom of the prisoners in Cyprus. Aimo was released from captivity in 1233 and soon restored to his family at Roccasecca. He was profoundly grateful to His Holiness and swore that forever afterward he would serve and support only the papal power. "Never again will I enlist with the Imperial army," he told Thomas when he visited the abbey for the first time after his release.

His mother was present, and she suggested firmly that he speak in hushed tones if he must say this at all in a public place. Thomas smiled from ear to ear. God is good, the elated younger brother reflected.

Thomas had three more years of calm in which to contemplate the goodness of God before the long and grasping Hohenstaufen arm found its way into his life again. Settling on the Abbey of Monte Cassino as a convenient tactical location for his campaign in Northern Sicily, the emperor stationed a garrison there. The stables and grounds provided ample room for his menagerie of exotic beasts, and the living quarters became housing for his personal harem. His soldiers forced the monks into servitude, ordering them to cut and haul wood, and to perform manual labor required for building their war machines.

"The Holy Roman Emperor, himself, has decreed it!" The captain of the guard snarled in response to the abbot's protests. "The monks will be responsible to supply at least half of what is needed for the sustenance of our soldiers and retinue. There is no gainsaying an imperial decree."

All semblance of order was lost, and the monks were finally forced to evacuate. Their newly appointed abbot, Stephen de Corbario, foresaw no relief from the violence and chaos afflicting the monastery. He urged Landolfo d'Aquino to remove his son to safety.

Abbot Corbario wrote to the count, outlining the situation at the abbey. He emphasized that Thomas' teachers were impressed with the quiet but inquisitive boy, who was diligent in his studies and unusually devout. The child seemed to be driven by intellectual curiosity to an extraordinary degree, frequently surprising the monks with profound questions that perplexed him such as "What is truth?" and "What *is* God?"

The other youths at the abbey liked him because of his kindliness, but Thomas spent most of his recreation time in the quiet of the abbey church. He preferred to bring his books there and immerse himself in its hospitable silence. Such eager intelligence as his, the abbot felt, should not be neglected. He suggested that Thomas be sent to live at the Benedictine monastery of San Demetrio in Naples. There he could live safely with the monks and further his studies at the only university Emperor Frederick would permit his subjects to attend, the *Studium Generale* at Naples.

"It seems the emperor's retinue in residence at Monte Cassino is wreaking havoc to an insupportable degree," Count d'Aquino told his wife, rubbing his forehead as he did when he was feeling weary.

"I was certain it would as soon as we heard of it," she said. "We must remove Tommaso at once. But what a pity—he has been thriving there."

"The new abbot, Corbario, suggests he be removed to the Benedictine monastery in Naples."

"San Demetrio? That is quite some distance from here." She considered a moment. "It will make visits more difficult."

"The abbot is convinced that our son must continue his studies. He confirms our impression that Tommaso has no ordinary intelligence. He feels the boy is equal to a higher level of education. At the *Studium Generale* in Naples he will have access to the most prominent teachers available, and the Benedictines will serve as his guardians and protectors."

"I suppose it is the best course both for him and for the Benedictines, if they are to be graced with an Aquino as abbot one day," she said, smiling. "He can learn a great deal there, no doubt. But," she hesitated, "his learning will be tainted with Imperial propaganda."

"True enough," the count agreed, "Still, the holy monks at San Demitrio are no fools. They will offer him guidance. And I believe the Holy Spirit will shield him as He has done in these past few turbulent years."

With his parents' consent, in the fall of 1239, the adolescent Thomas began his course of studies at the fledgling university founded and controlled directly by the Holy Roman Emperor. Although it was small in size, the emperor had appointed the best mentors academia had to offer. Its express purpose was to mold subjects fit for imperial service, loyal exclusively to himself and defiant of papal authority. Despite this dubious academic setting, the glimmer of truth and a misplaced gem caught Thomas' eye.

Chapter Three

THE MIND AND THE HEART OF THE MATTER

For the next five years, Thomas joined in the regular flow of religious life at the Monastery of San Demetrio along with other displaced monks from Monte Cassino. By contrast with the magnificent abbey he had left behind, this was a modest dwelling. Like most Neapolitan structures, the long narrow building was topped with a red tiled roof. It was attached to a small church barely taller than the three-story monastery. Worn to a yellowish brown by time and the saltwater that seasoned the harbor air, it was tucked away in an obscure corner of Naples, within an easy walking distance from the *Studium Generale*.

The two monasteries were different in more than appearance. The humble building in Naples housed an orderly existence, while the imposing crown of Monte Cassino had become a shell of chaos, long in a state of upheaval because of its precarious position in the midst of the political war. Thomas had always loved the Benedictine ideal and the integrity of life it was meant to foster, but he had seen little of that in the latter years at Monte Cassino. While the emperor's entourage resided within its walls, he witnessed a broad spectrum of moral corruption. The city of Naples, nestled beneath fuming Mount Vesuvius, had earned a reputation as a center of vice and crime. Yet within the monastery of San Demetrio, Thomas could focus on his studies and preserve the purity of heart that had been jolted amid the imperial storm.

His courses at the *Studium Generale* were in the liberal arts, as was typical of any university at that time. "Rigorously done," said Master Martin of Dacia, his logic professor, "the liberal arts build in the mind of the student the tools with which to reason well. That is the goal of your studies here." The professor was a slender man whose quick gestures accompanied his thoughts and punctuated his speech. Thrusting out a wiry hand, he explained, "With these tools firmly in place, each and every one of you will be equipped to seek out and grasp truth," and here he snapped his fist shut as if truth had been floating in the air, "wherever it can be found in the natural world." He raised his eyebrows meaningfully. Thomas liked him. "The ultimate goal of this education, men, is to reach the principles of nature, the 'first causes'."

It was a noble endeavor, as Master Martin described it. Thomas was eager.

"The humble beginning of the liberal arts, my friends, is the trivium: grammar, logic, and rhetoric." Master Martin enunciated each word distinctly, holding up one, two, three fingers on his right hand. "This means the study of language for the sake of reason and argument. The second component of the liberal arts is the quadrivium." Up went four fingers on his left hand, one after another, as he enumerated "the mathematically based sciences of arithmetic, geometry, astronomy, and music."

His keen eyes focused on each student in the room. "Their structured methodology will habituate your mind to think clearly, above all. Imitate their logic, my friends, and you will soon recognize the order inherent in all facets of the natural world!" He ended his lecture with an encouraging smile. His enthusiasm was irresistible.

With a mind ready and eager, Thomas progressed easily. For many of the students, Master Martin's zeal was their mainstay, keeping them on course as they worked their way through the difficult and sometimes dull technicalities of grammar and logic. Not so for Thomas whose zeal began where Master Martin's left off, although he manifested it more by hard work than by word or expression. His teachers, who were leaders in the academic world, took notice of his extraordinary memory and capacity for knowledge. He often seemed to surpass even his masters in depth of understanding.

"His appetite for learning, and his sense of wonder are tremendous," Master Martin told his colleague, the renowned Master Peter of Ireland, "although he generally keeps them hidden behind a curtain of shyness." Master Peter, known to his students as "the Hibernian," was a thickly built man with a fair complexion that flushed and blanched with his impassioned speech. On Martin's recommendation, he accepted Thomas early into his natural philosophy class. His assessment of the young Aquino concurred with Master Martin's. "The movements of his mind he can make crystal clear—when called upon; but those of his soul remain hidden." He spoke wistfully, as though the movements of this student's soul must be something extraordinary.

Thomas' academic studies at the University of Naples were formative, having set in motion forces that worked profoundly within him. These were embodied in the work of two men: Aristotle, whose influence emanated from the pagan world of pre-Christian Greece, and Saint Dominic, whose influence seemed to emanate from the heart of God. To the perceptive eye of this eager youth they glittered like gold, but it was rough, unpolished gold, not obvious to all.

Only a short time before Thomas had begun his studies with the Benedictines, the work of the ancient Greek philosopher, Aristotle, had been banned at leading academic institutions. At the preeminent University of Paris, students of the liberal arts were forbidden to study his large body of writing because some of its philosophical conclusions appeared to be contrary to fundamental tenets of Christianity.

The Bishop of Paris, speaking out of genuine concern, advised the consortium of masters at that university: "It seems most unwise to expose our impressionable young scholars to ideas that may be flawed and, at the same time, beyond their abilities to critique. Youth are excitable and, in their inexperience, quick to make judgments. It might well lead them astray." The rector of the University of Paris, as well as the majority of masters, concurred: "The work of the Stagirite is only suitable to mature thinkers, it may be harmful at this volatile level of education." Most institutions of higher education followed the example of the University of Paris and shunned the work of Aristotle.

By the time Thomas entered the *Studium Generale*, however, the ban had been cautiously lifted in Paris, due to the undeniable merit of Aristotle's work. At the fledgling University of Naples, where Thomas was living, the work of the pagan philosopher was positively embraced. Frederick II was vehement, "It has served the 'infidels' these many hundreds of years, and it served Alexander the Great before that. If it sufficed for those thinkers," the emperor insisted, "it surely suffices for our neophyte scholars." The absurdity of any other course of action caused his temper to flare. "We will not be jerked up and down, this way and that, by papal puppeteers!" This Holy Roman Emperor had no compunction whatever about exposing his students to allegedly anti-Christian thinkers. On the contrary, to his mind, the avant-garde quality added to its charm.

As a result, Aristotle's rediscovered work on logic, *The Organon*, served as the foundational text from which Thomas was educated. Master Martin of Dacia and Master Peter of Ireland, as well as most of their colleagues at the university, relied heavily upon it to explain, illustrate, and illumine their lectures. The students were well aware of the merit of the philosopher's work; its breadth and depth commanded their respect, and their masters made sure that it did not escape them.

As Master of Natural Philosophy, the Hibernian's admiration for the work of Aristotle was reverential, and he shared it with his class: "Aristotle originated in Stagira, an ancient Macedonian city of little significance," he said. "Yet, so great was his reputation for learning that the king of Macedonia summoned him to tutor his own son, Prince Alexander, in philosophy, government, politics, and poetry." The Hibernian's color rose as he grew more animated. "*After* the young prince had inherited the throne of his father and assumed the title, king of Macedonia, *after* he had overthrown the Persian empire, *after* he had conquered the *entire world* as far as the Indian Ocean and wept at the realization that there were no more lands to conquer," Master Peter's pale blue eyes widened in his ruddy face, "Alexander the Great still placed *more value* in the wisdom gleaned from his mentor than in *all* his other possessions."

Nodding his grizzled head approvingly, he paused in the narrative to allow the import of his words to penetrate. He then continued, "Although he had the entire known world at his disposal, King Alexander did not like to share that treasury of knowledge. Upon hearing that Aristotle was publishing his work—the very work we are studying now…" with a glance he indicated the manuscript on the tall wooden table beside him, "the young king became indignant and upbraided his tutor by letter for making his store of knowledge public! 'For what is there now that we excel others in,' the conqueror of the world demanded, 'if those things which we have been particularly instructed in be laid open to all? For my part,' the king had written, 'I assure you, I had rather excel others in the knowledge of what is excellent, than in the extent of my power and dominion.'" The Hibernian never tired of repeating this vignette as a testimony to the treasury of knowledge his students in Naples were privileged to study.

Although Alexander the Great was loathe to share it, Aristotle's work was soon discovered by other thinkers who grappled with the same issues and ideas. "It was wisdom gleaned from long years of study and discussion at Aristotle's Athenian school, the Lyceum," Master Peter explained. "Every topic had been treated there with a scrutiny born of genuine wonder, and intellectual discipline instilled by the same liberal arts that we are studying here at Naples—the trivium and the quadrivium." He paused again, briefly. "But it did not end there, no! Aristotle and his students pursued a myriad of topics to a degree only accessible to an educated mind. Any topic that captured their interest was subject to their investigation, from botany and marine biology to poetry, politics, ethics, and metaphysics. They were searching out and deciphering the natural order in the world!"

Thomas was happy to delve into the work of this great mind, which until his generation had been all but forgotten in the western world. From his reading at Monte Cassino, he knew that for hundreds of years after the collapse of the Roman Empire, Aristotle's work was lost to the West. It had fallen into the hands of the conquering Muslims and become the exclusive property of Eastern philosophers.

The most notable of these Islamic philosophers was a man called Abu al-Walid Muhammad Ahmad ibn Muhammad ibn Rushd. Latin scholars, and the Masters at the *Studium*, referred to him simply as Averroes. At the request of his caliph, Averroes wrote commentaries on most of Aristotle's work. It was actually Averroes' commentaries to which Thomas' professors in Naples had access.

Although it was not without merit, Averroes' writing was tainted with his cultural prejudices and cloudy reasoning. Misunderstanding, or misconstruing, the original intention of the author in subtle ways, he led would-be disciples of Aristotle astray. It was really his faulty interpretations that gave the impression of unorthodoxy to Aristotle's work. But Thomas thought he could see through the errors of the interpreter to the tantalizing truths beneath.

"Aristotle clearly maintained that truth is universal and whole, just as we do," Thomas explained, to the relief of his friend Dom Bernard Ayglier, a Benedictine from Lyon. The two made their way along the twisting half mile of cobbled streets from the *Studium* back to the abbey of San Demetrio. "It was Averroes— centuries later—who believed in a double truth: philosophical, on the one hand, and religious, on the other. Philosophical truth, to him, was supreme. It was the mystical property of the intellectual elite. Religious truth was merely useful and symbolic but often contradicted the profound truth of philosophy."

Dom Bernard nodded. "It is true, then, that the Eastern philosopher, Averroes, and not Aristotle, maintained that both philosophical and religious truths serve a purpose," he said, "and that somehow both are 'true' simultaneously, even when they conflict?"

"Yes," said Thomas. "And Averroes—contrary to Aristotle—believed that the human intellect is universal, not individual. He thought that individual minds merely participate in it."

"If that were so," Dom Bernard objected, "there could be no individual knower. No one could truly say, 'I think...' Is that not so?"

"Exactly so," agreed Thomas. "Aristotle, on the other hand, saw plainly that each individual has a distinct mind with which to assent to or reject ideas. His account is more in conformity with our experience of knowledge."

The confusions that had troubled Dom Bernard were the same ones that afflicted much of the academic community at that time. Many attributed Averroes' understanding to Aristotle, and condemned it, or at least viewed it with suspicion. The conclusions he drew directly contradicted common experience and the revealed truths central to Christianity. Averroes was obviously flawed, and so his commentaries were set aside by many Christian thinkers, along with the texts upon which he commented. Consequently, Aristotle's work fell into the shadows.

But in Naples, Frederick II's Muslim sympathies and combative instincts made even Averroes acceptable. There, Thomas and his peers were thoroughly exposed to the works of Aristotle as seen through the lens of Averroes. Yet Thomas' agile mind was able to sift out the mistakes made by Averroes and to revel in the wisdom of Aristotle. Thomas knew that truth is one, not divided or internally contradictory, as Averroes thought. Through the work of Aristotle, Thomas saw a way to unite the truths of faith with the truths of reason. Aristotle supplied the link. Rightly understood, philosophy could serve as a "handmaid" to theology.

At the same time that he was chiseling out the intellectual treasure he had found, another shaft of light caught his eye—this one penetrated his heart. For as long as Thomas could remember, he harbored a deep love of God and of all things pertaining to Him. Even his relentless appetite for truth sprang from the conviction that God is truth and all truth originates in God. A profound and abiding love permeated his being. The early years he had spent at Monte Cassino and his more recent years at San Demetrio had provided the opportunity to reflect on the meaning of this love. Now he faced it directly and found it to be substantial and eminently worthwhile. He longed to spend his life in service to it. In Naples, he discovered the path by which he could.

Not far from the Benedictine Monastery of San Demetrio where Thomas lived, was the small priory of San Domenico Maggiore. Thomas befriended the only two men who lived there, Friar Thomas of Lentini and Friar John of San Giuliano. The rest of their mendicant brothers had been expelled by Frederick II, but these two remained behind to teach theology at Frederick's *Studium Universale*. Any respectable university included courses in theology, and so the men were tolerated by the Holy Roman Emperor.

In the conspicuous black and white robes of their order, they taught, studied, and went about the work they had given their lives to: leading souls to God. Thomas found their obvious joy irresistible. Like Thomas, they recognized the power of truth to draw people into a deeper love of God. Theirs was the ideal enunciated by Jesus in the temple at Jerusalem 1,200 years before: "You will know the truth, and the truth will set you free."

These men were authentic Catholic priests following as closely as they could in the footsteps of Christ. Their religious order had been established only thirty years earlier by Dominic de Guzman, a brilliant and holy man whose example inspired them and whose wisdom guided them. They were "the Dominicans."

Thirty years before Thomas encountered the Dominicans in the streets of Naples, the founder of their order, Friar Dominic, had recognized a need to clarify the doctrines of Christianity for Christians in every walk of life. In his efforts to teach, he had heard a distressing degree of misunderstanding among well-meaning people, and wanted to share with them the richness and reasonableness of the faith he loved. That could only be done well, he thought, by living a life of prayer, virtue, and study. Those were, he believed, the indispensable tools of effective preaching. Soon, many other men and women joined him in his apostolate. Finally, word of their work reached Pope Honorius III.

Educating the clergy and, through them, all Christians, in a firm foundation of truth was a cause close to the heart of that pontiff. He understood the priceless treasure that lay in the teaching of Christ and took seriously the commission to the apostles and their successors to "teach all nations."

As a vicar of Christ on earth, he encouraged those who shared this conviction. He offered the growing community of Dominicans a residence in Rome and approved their work. "They are champions of the faith and true lights of the world," he declared. After only a few years, he gave Dominic his blessing to establish the Order of Preachers, the Dominicans.

Thomas felt himself irresistibly drawn to the life of prayer and study. He longed to be a Dominican. Although he was well aware that it did not accord with his family's ambitions, Thomas was convinced that he was called to this new religious order.

In April of 1244, at the Dominican priory of San Domenico in Naples, Thomas took the habit of the Dominican Order of Friars Preachers, professing his intention before Prior Thomas Lentini to live the life of a mendicant; to study, to pray, to renounce worldly goods, and to obey the Dominican rule. In his commitment to a life of single-hearted service to God, Thomas was at peace.

His mother, however, was not.

Chapter Four

REFINED LIKE SILVER, TESTED LIKE GOLD

Theodora's husband, Count Landolfo, who was nearly two decades her senior, had passed away only the year before, in 1243. Perhaps he would have tolerated these caprices of their son, but the responsibility for the family's honor now rested on her shoulders, and she was furious.

These were indeed trying times for the family d'Aquino. When news first reached her that her youngest son had thrown away his chances of a respectable career with the Benedictines and joined that radical new religious order, she resolved to stop him. She was anxious, too, because Frederick II despised the mendicants and had recently banished all but a handful from the imperial territories. A faithful subject would not take the habit of a banned order. Lady Theodora knew well that Frederick II was not lightly crossed. In fact, all the world knew it.

At this very time, people who dared defy Frederick in the town of Viterbo, just north of Rome, experienced his wrath. Viterbo had been a long-suffering ally of the emperor, but finally its citizens could endure his oppressive stranglehold no longer.

"They have imprisoned the imperial governor of Viterbo, Simon of Chieti, and his guard of four hundred German knights," the countess informed her family at Roccasecca one evening in the spring of 1244. She had spent that day in Aquino with her late husband's cousin, the Count of Acerra, attending to the affairs of her estate.

"Any uprising that affects the Two Sicilies must weigh heavily upon poor Sir Thomas, as viceroy to the Emperor," Marrotta said.

"Yes, indeed," her mother agreed. "He spoke of little else."

"Where do you suppose they put all those knights?" Theodora wondered.

"The irony is too much!" her mother answered. "They locked the entire guard within the walls of that ostentatious castle that Frederick himself had built in the town at incredible cost." Lady Theodora smiled wryly. "That is one way of getting their taxes back."

Aimo was well aware of the situation. "The Viterbians were irate. They swarmed the guards forcing them into the castle, shouting all the while, 'Long live the Pope,' 'Death to Count Simon!'"

The countess caught her breath. "I wonder how that will sit with His Imperial Highness?"

"It will not 'sit' at all. He is already gathering his forces to retaliate," said Aimo ominously.

Thus began the city's historic revolt. The rest of Italy watched with awe and took heart from the courage of Viterbo as word of its treason reached and infuriated Frederick in Tuscany. While the emperor prepared to retaliate, Viterbians geared up for the inevitable arrival of his forces, and shock waves from their rebellion rocked the country.

The Holy Father at this time, Innocent IV, financed reinforcing troops to aid the Viterbians. Rome formed an alliance with Viterbo and promised military aid. All over the country, victims of imperial oppression cautiously shed their shackles, wrongs were righted, ill-gotten papal lands were restored, and papal support gained momentum. Then all eyes turned to Viterbo as Frederick descended on it with a vengeance.

In the angry onslaught that followed, two knights of the house of Aquino rode under the banner of the emperor: Thomas' own brothers, Landolfo and Rinaldo, in the faithful service of their Lord Hohenstaufen. Justice would be swift, they thought like their lord, and soon the Viterbians and all of Italy would realize the folly of defiance.

But they were mistaken. Viterbo was fighting for its life with a resistance born of desperation. After months of surprising back-to-back defeats, Frederick and his men were forced to pause, and they took a respite in nearby Acquapendente.

Resting there with the beleaguered imperial troops, Landolfo and Rinaldo received word from home of young Thomas' act of rebellion. They did some investigating and soon discovered that out of fear of the noble Aquinos, the Dominicans had removed Thomas from Naples and taken him north, but his family knew not where. Their mother sent a courier to enlist the help of her two sons to find and return him.

Frederick II gave the two Aquinos permission to go with a small band of soldiers in search of their wayward brother. Along with them, he sent his own imperial counselor, Pietro del Vigne. In that company, he knew, their mission would be swift and sure. It could not possibly fail. "We depart on the morrow," Landolfo informed his mother by letter, "with the emperor's caveat to make haste. The presence of Del Vigne is a great boon. Our success is assured."

So it was that later that month in Acquapendente, Frederick II held audience with the indignant master general of the Dominicans, John von Wildeshausen, and a disheveled looking youth with incongruously calm brown eyes. The newly professed Tommaso d'Aquino had been abducted by the imperial contingent as he traveled with his Dominican superior on the road from Rome to Bologna. Uninvited, John von Wildeshausen accompanied them to the camp, vehemently protesting the use of physical force on one of his novices.

John von Wildeshausen was a compatriot of Emperor Frederick Hohenstaufen; they had been friends in their youth. Before encountering the Dominicans, he had spent several years in Frederick's court in Germany. He hoped that out of past friendship, at least, Frederick might order Thomas' release. But Frederick had agreed to the abduction in the first place and contributed aid toward its accomplishment. To relent would be a display of weakness, something he rejected as unthinkable.

For his part, Rinaldo explained his intent to expose this sheltered youngest brother to the real world; the exhilarating life of power and passion as it was played out in the imperial service. Frederick gave his blessing to Rinaldo and Landolfo. Von Wildeshausen's protests were entirely ignored and he was sent away alone to the general chapter of Dominicans in Bologna. Thomas was taken under guard to the family's more remote castle at Monte San Giovanni, sixteen miles north of Roccasecca.

Thomas was silent but not sullen with the soldiers who escorted him. They made their way over the hills and mountains to Monte San Germano, a fortress within the papal states that His Holiness, Adrian IV, had bestowed on the family d'Aquino some hundred years previously. His brothers dispatched a courier to inform their mother that they had Thomas in tow and would bring him to Roccasecca soon. In the meantime, they were concocting a plot to destroy the pious sentiments that shielded Thomas from worldly corruption. They would expose him to everything he had renounced. If he was human, they thought, he would not be able to resist—it would be a lesson he would not forget. Leaving Thomas under guard, they attended to the details of their plan.

The imperial soldiers held him in a cell in the Aquino's fortress tower until his brothers returned. After the soldiers departed, Landolfo and Rinaldo set to work. Their first assault was one of words. With all the eloquence they could muster, they urged him to give up his sanctimonious notions and instead join them in the exhilarating world of action and prestige. They lectured him, they tried to entice him, they argued with him. They appealed to his sense of family honor, describing the attractions of their way of life and gnawing at his resolve in every way they could.

None of it swayed Thomas. He listened, shook his head, and smiled wearily, but he would not give in. When they had reached the end of their scanty patience, the brothers decided to unleash on Thomas what they considered to be their ultimate weapon.

Late that night, the stillness of the fortress was broken by a wail of profound anguish, bellowing from the heart of one who had endured too much in long-suffering silence. Within minutes, Rinaldo and Landolfo were outside the door of Thomas' cell as it flew open to reveal the giant youth in Dominican robes furiously wielding a flaming brand in front of a pale young woman as she backed out of the room. Shaking with terror and indignation, the woman spat contemptuously at the elder brothers and ran past them. The door to Thomas' cell slammed closed and the sound of the brand scraping its surface was audible as it etched the form of a cross into the wood.

The brothers now realized their folly. They had hired this woman who had no scruples against seducing young men, religious or otherwise. While Thomas slept, they had ushered her into his cell and left her to practice her trade. Their hope was that if anyone could break his resolve, it would be this beautiful woman. She would be able to lure him to violate his vows and embrace the pleasures of the world in a way he had not yet encountered. Now they saw that they had utterly misjudged Tommaso.

The next morning, the three young men traveled to Roccasecca in strained silence. Their mother, unaware of the unsavory tactics employed by her two elder sons, welcomed them gratefully and took Thomas aside for a severe scolding.

"I am gravely disappointed in you, Tommaso," she said sternly. "You have shown no consideration for your family. You have disregarded our wishes, and despised our efforts spent on your upbringing and education. You have cast off a fine future and exposed the entire family to the real possibility of imperial disfavor. This is no light matter. I am provoked beyond measure."

Thomas mumbled an apology for causing her distress. He was very tired, and genuinely grieved, but he remained firm. He spoke, alluding to the passage in Scripture which reads, "Seek ye the Lord where he may be found," and "Your ways are not my ways, saith the Lord."

The only encouragement he received was the shadow of a sympathetic smile from the steward, Mazzeo, who could not help but overhear the charged exchange. Lady Theodora refused to understand her son's meaning.

"I do not believe the Lord's ways include open defiance of your mother! Nor do I believe that God has abandoned the Benedictines to reside exclusively among the religious rabble," she fumed. Thomas said no more.

Finding him intractable, she confined him to his room to reconsider and relent. She was prepared to keep him there as long as it took for his zeal to cool so that he could see the situation as she so clearly saw it. No Aquino should stoop to the level of a begging preacher. If he were determined to become a monk, he could do so in the respectable cloister of nearby Monte Cassino. Peace had returned there now, and his own father had financed most of the abbey's restoration after the damage it had suffered from Frederick's garrison. There, her son could wield influence and bring honor to the name of Aquino. As a member of the Dominican order, on the other hand, he would be in the disfavor of the Holy Roman Emperor, he would probably be exiled from the imperial territories, and would most surely cast a shadow of doubt on the family's fidelity. In subsequent months, Lady Theodora kept her youngest son confined at home. Landolfo and Rinaldo bid a sheepish goodbye and returned to what they understood, the imperial siege of Viterbo. Although the countess' sympathies were with the Viterbians in that conflict, she feared for her soldier sons and knew she could not object to their participation in the assault. They were knights in service to the king. So be it.

At Roccasecca, Thomas was allowed to read, pray, write and converse with his sisters. The animosity that initially seasoned his abduction soon diminished. In the first few weeks, his sisters visited Thomas in his cell with the intention of changing his mind. One after another, they urged him to obey their mother and relinquish his obstinacy. He would shame the family, he might attract the emperor's frightening displeasure; at the very least he would be exiled. Furthermore, all this was unnecessary, they said. He could simply return to Monte Cassino and live the life of a monk where it was socially acceptable and advantageously close to home.

But with time, Thomas was able to reveal to them the irresistible love that moved him, how it manifested in the truth he had been studying, how he longed to search out that truth for the great good it was, and the great good it could accomplish in the hearts of others. With the Dominicans, he explained, he would be able to devote himself wholly to it. The Dominicans practiced the evangelical counsels of poverty, chastity, and obedience faithfully; they were entirely devoid of worldly ambition, and the study of divine truth was fundamental to their constitution.

His eldest sister, Marrotta, was the first to begin to understand him, to see something of what he saw. She stopped urging Thomas to deny his heart and began gently to suggest to their mother that they may have been wrong. Thomas was not acting out of impulse or defiance, she now realized, but out of an instinct perhaps they had no right to tamper with. Eventually, they all became aware of Thomas' sincere conviction and his extraordinary appetite for learning. He had a natural facility for communicating what he understood to the minds of those who would listen.

Friar John of San Giuliano, his friend from the priory at Naples, had long before recognized an uncommon intensity of mind and heart in the young Aquino nobleman. He knew where this young man belonged. The Dominicans would not abandon him, and he, personally, would make that plain.

As soon as he heard of Thomas' abduction, Friar John found his way to the *rocca*. He waited on the grounds outside the castle daily to show support to the captive and humble defiance to the captors. He took whatever opportunities arose to come inside and pay a visit. When Lady Theodora became aware of this, she received him with cool reserve. But he came anyway, to encourage Thomas, to nourish his intellect with conversation and his soul with spiritual guidance. He brought news, too, of the world and of his fellow Dominicans.

The countess could only throw up her hands and even laugh—a little—when she noticed that Friar John always arrived looking overstuffed, wearing two fresh, clean Dominican habits. The lower layer was obviously his own, but the outer layer was clearly not, with its bulk carefully folded and tucked wherever possible. But he always left the castle still wearing his own clean habit, and enveloped in yet another that was clearly worn, wrinkled and vastly too large. At the same time, Thomas' habit underwent an improving transformation. It was a harmless intrigue, she decided, and it saved her the trouble of insisting that her son take the absurd thing off if only for laundering. His brothers, she knew, had tried to remove it forcibly when they first found him on the *Via Latina*, and they came home with bruises to show for it.

Besides exchanging robes, the two men exchanged ideas: thoughts about philosophical and theological issues, quandaries they had with texts they had both read. Friar John told Thomas a little about the happenings in the world and among their mutual friends. More than anything else, they prayed together, and spoke with awe about the things of God.

Friar John brought Thomas a copy of *The Sentences* of Peter Lombard, the compendium of theological wisdom used by all students of theology. For Thomas, *The Sentences* had an effect something like a polish, scouring tarnish from the mind to open it to the luster of Sacred Scripture. Within its pages, the thoughts of the best Christian writers were brought to bear on questions about the nature of God and his goodness, mercy, and love. It addressed the meaning of the mission of the Son of God made man. And it gave an accounting of the place of humanity in the world.

In his long hours of confinement, Thomas committed both the Bible and *The Sentences* to memory. With these two books, and whatever texts of Aristotle he could obtain through Friar John, Thomas used his protracted stay at home to study and write essays for his friends at Naples. When his sisters came in with food, they usually stayed to talk. Thomas knew so much that they had never heard before, and he expressed it all in such a clear and beautiful way. More and more frequently, they came to visit him.

Late in July of the year 1245, Rinaldo arrived at the *rocca* stealthily by night. Fatigued and on edge, he told his family about the current political situation, which was volatile. He and Landolfo had been with the imperial forces in northern Italy the previous month, where Frederick was fomenting a civil war in the city of Narni while attempting to come to diplomatic terms with the newest pope's intermediaries. Under the threat of imperial invasion, real or imagined, Pope Innocent IV had fled to Lyons, France.

Accompanied by popular sympathy, the pope called an ecumenical council to address the problems of the day. Foremost among them: the unrelenting tyranny of Frederick II. At the council, which took place within months of his arrival in Lyons, he addressed the sufferings the Church was enduring at the hands of the Saracens abroad, and of Frederick II at home. He was presented with irrefutable evidence of the civil and moral crimes of which Frederick was widely accused. In less than three weeks, the Holy Father drew his conclusions and issued his sentence, one such as no other pope before or since had ever had the authority—or the audacity—to declare.

Pope Innocent IV enumerated the oaths the emperor had broken, the injustices he had inflicted on his vassals, the cruel revenge he had meted out to cities sympathetic with the pope, the churches he had raided, the men and women he had dismembered, the murders and assassinations for which he was responsible, the unlawful alliances, the abuses committed against even his own Saracen contingents, his attacks on Christians and on Christianity, and the criminal neglect of the poor and needy in his kingdoms. Solemnly, Innocent IV declared Frederick II unworthy of the crown and, with "the aim…of healing and not death, correction and not destruction," he excommunicated him.

Even more poignant for the devoutly Catholic family of Aquino was the decree by His Holiness that this declaration of excommunication extended to any who aided or cooperated with Frederick II from that day forward.

"We absolve from their oath forever all those who are bound to him by an oath of loyalty, firmly forbidding by our apostolic authority anyone in the future to obey or heed him as emperor or king, and decreeing that anyone who henceforth offers advice, help or favor to him as to an emperor or king, automatically incurs excommunication," the Holy Father unflinchingly declared.

The empire responded to this dramatic event with fear and confusion. To deny Frederick was death, to serve him was eternal death. While in his service, the Aquinos already had grave misgivings about many of his dealings, but felt they were not free to withdraw. Now, at last, the line was clearly drawn.

Rinaldo and Landolfo, together in Turin, witnessed Frederick's outraged reception of the pope's decree. In the tense silence of the assembly hall, the indignant monarch screamed, "I have not yet lost my crowns!" He demanded the treasure coffers that held his several crowns. When they were unlocked and set before him, he looked defiantly about the room and declared, "See if my crowns are lost now!"

Taking up one of the crowns, he held it over his head and, shaking with rage, declared, "I have not yet lost my crown and it shall cost the pope and the council a bloody struggle before they rob me of it. Does he, in his vulgar pride, think that he shall hurl me from the Imperial dignity? I, who am the chief Prince of the world, yea, who am without an equal?"

He paused to scour the faces of stupefied onlookers for anyone who dared look him in the eye or who, once looking, dared to turn away. "But it is all the better for me," he hissed through clenched teeth. "I was bound before to respect him in some things, but now I am set free from all ties of love or peace."

Rinaldo and Landolfo, once so brash in the emperor's service, could no longer hold up their heads and meet him eye-to-eye. At the first opportunity, Rinaldo slipped away on pretense of aiding his fatherless family. Landolfo remained reluctantly and dangerously situated among the imperial forces in Northern Italy. Both Aquino knights searched for a credible excuse to remove themselves far from Frederick's watchful eye.

In the days that followed Rinaldo's return to Roccasecca, the family focused intensely on what they should do. Their position was precarious but their priorities were now clear. Frederick had overstepped his legitimate authority. Rinaldo had sworn fealty to Frederick II, and was uneasy, to say the least, about leaving his service. Even apart from the obvious concern for his and Landolfo's safety, was it right for a soldier to abandon his post? The idea was abhorrent.

The Aquinos debated the matter with trepidation. Terrible possibilities weighed in the balance. Thomas had already given this question a great deal of thought, particularly to the issue of obedience, "as in the obligations of a son toward his mother."

"In most things," he told Rinaldo, "obviously, a soldier must obey his commander. Justice requires it." Their mother, who was listening, readily assented.

"Without that, there would be no order," agreed Rinaldo, "and anarchy would surely ensue."

"Yet, in some situations a subject may *not* be bound to obey his superior," Thomas said.

"Namely?" asked Theodora, paying close attention.

"Namely, when there is a still higher power to which one is subject," Thomas answered. "What if a commissioner issues an order that is contrary to the bidding of the proconsul—are you to comply with it?

"Certainly not, and no one would expect it," answered Rinaldo.

"And, if the proconsul commanded one thing, and the emperor another, will you hesitate to disregard the former and serve the latter?"

"Not a mite," the soldier replied, "and I see where this is leading."

"So do I!" interrupted Theodora. "If the emperor commands one thing and God another, you must disregard the former and obey God."

Thomas smiled at his sister, whose bright eyes had always reflected her quick wits.

"The logic is plain enough," their mother said, "but I am deeply apprehensive of the consequences."

"As am I," Thomas said.

"As are we all," Aimo added.

"Nevertheless, it cannot be denied that Frederick has commanded his soldiers to act contrary to their consciences, contrary to *God's law* as it is written in their hearts. By that fact alone they are not bound to obey Frederick."

"I suppose that is why Pope Innocent extended the excommunication to anyone who cooperates with him," Rinaldo added grimly.

"And now that the Holy Father, speaking as a higher authority, has asked his subjects to disregard the lesser authority—the emperor—they are bound to obey *him*," said Marrotta, taking up the thread of conversation.

"The principle is that a subject is bound to obey his superior only within the sphere of his authority," said Thomas. "Since Pope Innocent's decree, Frederick no longer has the authority to command his knights."

He turned to his mother. "By that same principle," he said gently, "neither is a child bound to obey his parents in spiritual matters if they direct him to act contrary to the will of God."

In the end, it was decided that Rinaldo should return to northern Italy, ostensibly in the service of Frederick. There he would work with Landolfo to aid the Holy Father's efforts and, at the same time—God willing—the two young men would contrive a safe means of escape that would not draw the emperor's disfavor on the family.

Lady Theodora watched her soldier son ride away, and with ambivalence lifted the interdict against her mendicant son. She did not explicitly permit him to leave. But she was sufficiently chastened by his counsel and the evolving political situation to turn a blind eye when Friar John arrived one evening with a rope and basket to maneuver a Pauline-style escape from Thomas' tower cell.

Almost two years after being taken captive by his family, Thomas was restored to his Dominican confreres in Naples. He then went on to Rome, where he was reunited with John von Wildeshausen, who was beside himself with joy at Thomas' return.

In the venerable company of the master general, Thomas traveled to Paris. The two were welcomed at the spacious new Dominican priory of Saint Jacques on rue Saint-Benoit near the University of Paris. At last, he commenced his long-delayed novitiate year.

While Thomas' return to his chosen life was sweet, Rinaldo's return to his once-sweet life was bitter. The only course left to Rinaldo was charged with peril. In his absence, he learned that Landolfo had been dispatched and no one could tell him for certain where he was. In that brief lapse of time, Frederick had sent a diplomatic delegation to Paris to appeal to King Louis IX for his intercession with Pope Innocent. Perhaps Landolfo had gone as guard to the Parisian contingent? At the same time, Frederick had assigned a military escort to some Venetian diplomats who had been in Turin to offer obeisance. Landolfo might be with that cohort. Or, most likely, he had accompanied King Conrad across the Alps.

King Conrad, Frederick's eldest legitimate son, had been traveling for months in his father's company, imbibing

Hohenstaufen power and diplomacy-in-action like a political suckling. For his return to Germany, his father had contributed money and a large array of imperial knights. It was quite possible that Landolfo was among those luckless soldiers.

Frederick was much too occupied with his deteriorating empire to concern himself with Rinaldo's search for his brother, nor was Rinaldo eager to attract the emperor's attention. By this time, Rinaldo's conversion was complete. He saw plainly that Frederick, whom he had served since childhood, first as a page and finally as a knight, had now become an agent for the forces of evil. He realized, too, that the Holy Father was trying to combat that evil. He ardently hoped that his path and Landolfo's would somehow cross. But if that was not to be in this life, he was determined to ensure their reunion in the next. He would serve only one master from here on—the Divine Master.

In the manner of a soldier, his resolve quickly turned to deeds. He made clandestine contact with a large group of compatriots in northern Italy. The conspirators desperately hoped to find a way to rid the country of the deposed monarch and restore order to their tyrannized land.

All hope was quickly lost, however, when the Argus-like Frederick discovered a smaller plot against his life and that of his illegitimate son, Enzio. As King of Sardinia, Enzio had perpetrated a brutal siege at Parma. As if driven to prove himself every bit a Hohenstaufen, he had inflicted cruelties on the inhabitants worthy of his father. No love was wasted in Parma on this offspring of the "Wonder of the World." At the Abbey of Fontana Viva, where Frederick stopped on the road to Parma, he came across some papers in the library revealing the plot. The coincidence seemed like a diabolically orchestrated nightmare, the effect of which was brutally real. Many of the suspected conspirators fled, a few were exiled, the rest were executed.

Within a few weeks, a wider and more devastating plot was uncovered among the ranks of the emperor's own knights. The emperor was beside himself. Men he had trusted, relied upon, and to whom he had vouchsafed great honors, were stealthily planning his demise. As his paranoia reached fever pitch, his self-control unraveled. Any conspirators, suspected conspirators, or children of suspected conspirators that he could find were murdered on the spot. He locked up their wives in a windowless dungeon without food or water and never released them. Many terrified suspects fled to scattered fortresses. Some were guilty, some were innocent, but all dreaded the wrath of Frederick Hohenstaufen.

A desperate contingent of nobles took refuge at Capaccio, an almost impenetrable fortress in southwestern Italy far from Frederick's camp, but the distance was not great enough to protect them. Frederick descended upon Capaccio with a crazed vengeance. His siege engines battered the pipes, the cisterns, and the walls of the fortress ceaselessly day and night. When the hostages finally yielded, they were gathered up and publicly mutilated.

With their eyes gouged out, and hands, feet, and noses cut off, the victims were paraded throughout the kingdom of the Two Sicilies while they bled to death or succumbed to gangrene. The imperial criers proclaimed, *"Behold the punishment of a monster, so that you may infer the doom of men, who like brute animals have plotted the death of him that made them. Behold the monster, and forget not his just sentence."*

Rinaldo d'Aquino was among the knights executed in that Capaccio siege. Landolfo was never found.

~

Thomas had been uneasy about both of his brothers ever since Rinaldo left Roccasecca. News of their fates did not reach Thomas in Paris or his apprehensive family at home for many months, long after the *fait accompli*.

As rumors circulated in Paris of the brutal siege at Capaccio, Thomas was filled with foreboding. He seemed to know that the siege had personal meaning, and a tremendous weight descended upon his breast. It troubled his sleep and his solitary moments. It permeated his prayers. He did not speak of it, but the anxiety in his usually serene features was faintly visible. Something deep within his brown eyes hinted of pain.

One early morning before the day's heat had lifted the dew, a courier from the house of Aquino arrived on horseback outside the priory gates on rue Saint-Benoit. Thomas was summoned from the chapel where he had spent most of the night in prayer.

"Your mother has sent me with a message," the courier's voice quavered. It was Mazzeo, whom Thomas had known since childhood. He was not just the Aquinos' steward, but a trusted family friend. When the children were small, Mazzeo taught Thomas, Adalasia and Mary how to play *calcio*, their favorite game. He had taken great pains to perfect their kicking and dodging skills so that they could keep up with their older brothers and sisters. Thomas recalled lively summer evenings spent on the castle grounds with Mazzeo and the other children, engrossed in the game. The recollection made him wince. Several years had passed since Thomas saw him last and time had made its inevitable mark, but the old steward's face was lined with more than age.

"My brothers are dead," Thomas intuited. The words were blunt, but softly spoken. His anguish was obvious.

The servant lost his self-mastery for a moment, his eyes filling with tears that quickly spilled over. Thomas placed a comforting arm across his shoulders and the two went out to the garden behind the priory. On a rustic bench outside they watched the sun rise and eventually reach its apex while they spoke of Rinaldo, Landolfo, and the grieving family at home.

The old steward told Thomas what he knew of Rinaldo's death. His information was sparse. Roger of San Severino, whose father was well known to their family, had been present at the siege of Cappacio, but had lost contact with Rinaldo during the attack. San Severino and a handful of men escaped. Rinaldo had not been so fortunate.

Angrily Mazzeo described the emperor's cruel treatment of the captives, halting over the impact of his words. Thomas listened, his heart beating hard. The burden of trepidation he had carried these many months tightened in his chest. Mazzeo spoke, too, of the unlikelihood of ever finding Landolfo. "We must assume he, too, is dead. For in Frederick's present state of mind, he would never allow Landolfo to live. There can be no doubt that if he did not meet his demise in active service, then our Landolfo has been executed as an accomplice." It was hard to hear these words. Thomas loved his brothers deeply; their cruel deaths opened a fresh wound in his heart.

His sympathy for the old servant sustained him through the painful interview. At the end, their conversation turned to the mysterious providence of God.

"It is difficult to fathom the ways of God," the servant said, looking at Thomas for some account that he could understand and cling to.

Thomas' answer came readily. "We must place our trust in His infinite goodness, Mazzeo," he murmured. "'He is a merciful and gracious God,' so say the Psalms. Although he allows men freedom to choose good or to inflict evil, he does not abandon his creatures for a moment. His mercy extends to everyone, to Landolfo, to Rinaldo, and to all of us who suffer for their sake."

Mazzeo hung his head as he listened. Thomas continued. "On the cross Our Lord suffered grievously out of the depths of His love for each and every one of us. The mercy won through that Divine suffering is not limited by time or place. We can be assured that it accompanied Rinaldo through his agony, and Landolfo through his." The confidence with which Thomas spoke seemed to spring from a hidden source, and it eased the pain of both men a little. "Now we must rely upon the same Divine mercy to carry us through our suffering. It is in suffering that we draw near to the infinite love of God, and there our hearts will find rest." He spoke as one who knows with certainty that what he says is true.

The old man finally left, having completed his bitter task. Alone again with his thoughts, Thomas returned directly to the cool stillness of the dimly lit chapel. The Dominican brothers at Saint Jacques were well aware of the unfolding of events by that time, and left him alone in the presence of God.

Kneeling upright on the bare stone floor before the Blessed Sacrament, his shoulders shook ever so slightly as tears coursed down his cheeks. He bowed his head. "All the ways of God are mercy and truth," he whispered. "I know this, and I accept Thy holy will."

With a heavy heart, he returned to his studies. His mind was not entirely at peace about his brothers until, one night many months later, he experienced a vivid dream reassuring him that both men were safely in the hands of God where the flames of Frederick's earthly hell could not touch them.

Chapter Five

FOUNDATIONS OF ROCK AND SAND

For the next three years, Thomas lived the Dominican ideal. He was immersed in prayer and study at the newly constructed priory of Saint Jacques along with more than one hundred other Dominican friars. The stately edifice was a gift of King Louis IX, built where a hostel for pilgrims *en route* to the shrine of Saint James at Compostella had formerly stood. Its domed chapel was still under construction but already dominated the landscape of the left-bank area near the Porte d'Orleans.

In this setting, time and the grace of God gently worked to dull the pain of loss he felt after the death of his brothers. Political upheaval began to seem remote and incongruous. In the first year, his formation focused on the intellectual and spiritual tradition of the ecclesial fathers. It was a delight to return to many of the same theologians he had learned about as a child at Monte Cassino. Now he could probe deeply into the minds of Augustine and Jerome, Tertullian and Cyprian.

Armed with the testimony of the intellectual giants, he made his solemn profession at the end of the term. Joyfully, he submitted himself to a life of contemplation through prayer and study, and to preaching through word and example. When he professed the evangelical counsels, the vows of poverty, chastity, and obedience, it was as if the words of Jesus to the rich young man of the Gospels—"Come, follow me"—were spoken directly to him, and he did not turn away.

In his second and third year, Thomas resumed the studies he had begun at the *Studium* in Naples, before he had taken the Dominican habit. He completed his courses in the liberal arts and began to study the *Nichomachean Ethics* of Aristotle.

"The man was a genius!" Thomas exclaimed out loud as he pored over these manuscripts in the university library. Two Dominican brothers reading at the same table glanced up. Seeing that he was speaking to himself, they exchanged tolerant glances and returned to their work. Thomas was oblivious to all but the manuscript on the table before him. Admiration burst out in audible words again. "He has formulated a science of human action!"

The *Nichomachean Ethics* was an intelligible account of the nature of human activity and the consequences of virtue and vice. In a collection of ten manuscripts written from lectures delivered by Aristotle himself at the Lyceum 1,600 years before, the whole purpose of human existence was explained.

"It all rings true," Thomas thought to himself as he made his way toward the mist-enveloped dome at the end of rue Saint-Benoit. It was almost time for vespers. The sinking sun barely penetrated the haze, and the gray of the river and the sky blended. Walking pensively along the street that extended from the Seine to the priory, Thomas was only sensible of his thoughts. "Happiness is, of course, what everyone longs for. That is the most fundamental cry of the human heart. Aristotle recognized that fact, and he realized that it spurs us on to everything we do."

Thomas reveled in the clarity of Aristotle's arguments. "Happiness is found in the perfection of human activity, and human activity is most perfect in the life of virtue. The life of virtue is fully realized in contemplation of the highest good! Even the pre-Christian pagans saw it, and what's more, here is a perfectly rational accounting," he reflected.

The importance of such a treatise was clear to Thomas. "One could hardly read it, and savor its wisdom, without being moved toward goodness," he thought as he turned in at the open gate to join the flow of black-and white-robed friars streaming toward the chapel doors. The bells of Saint-Jacques began to clang in the damp evening air, calling the brothers to vespers.

Only four or five feet in front of him as he entered the chapel doors that evening strode the one man who, Thomas knew, truly understood the genius of Aristotle. It was the respected German philosopher, Friar Albert of Lauingen. Thomas had been told that "Albert the Great," as he was widely referred to, was composing a commentary on Aristotle's *Ethics*. Like Thomas, Friar Albert recognized in Aristotle's *Ethics* a coherent science of human action, having its roots in universal and necessary principles.

How Thomas longed to talk to him, to glean the thoughts of so brilliant a mind about these manuscripts that he prized and pored over day and night. He began to study the writings and lectures of Albert, too, and to copy his manuscripts by hand. But he was too shy to approach him, so lofty did the great man seem.

Thomas had learned Albert's history easily enough. Everyone in Paris seemed to know him, or at least to know something about him. Twenty-five years earlier, the tall, elegant Bavarian nobleman, Albert of Lauingen, was a student of liberal arts in Padua. He was prominent in society and carried himself with comfortable assurance. Life changed for Albert, however, when he encountered Jordan of Saxony, the charismatic master general of the Dominicans at that time. Friar Jordan had come to the university town of Padua to explain the foundation of his faith to any who would listen.

"Friar Jordan spoke 'with the tongues of angels'," Thomas once overheard Albert say. "The combination of his conviction and wisdom was irresistible. In my years at Padua, more than one thousand students and teachers sought to enter the new Order of Preachers because of this one man's eloquence, and his obvious goodness."

Albert's heart had been set aflame by the preaching of Jordan of Saxony. Through the inspiration of Friar Jordon and, Albert always insisted, through the miraculous intervention of the Mother of God, Albert was moved to leave the world behind and take the Dominican habit. Like Thomas, Albert never looked back.

As a religious in the Order of Preachers, he prayed and studied; he wrote and lectured; he used all of his prodigious talents to bring the truth to light. He taught theology, but the subjects that interested him were numerous. He wrote about the sciences, from mineralogy to astronomy, and about each division of philosophy: natural, moral and metaphysical. He felt strongly that reason could be, and indeed must be, applied to every branch of knowledge, including the study of sacred things.

When Thomas arrived at the University of Paris in 1245, Albert had just received his doctorate and appointed a master in theology. He lived at the Dominican priory on rue Saint-Benoit, and often lectured there. The respect that his tall and imposing appearance commanded was nothing compared to the awe inspired by the workings of his expansive mind. In the academic world, his contemporaries referred to him as the Universal Doctor, because of his broad range of knowledge and his zeal for awakening others to the wonders of nature and reason.

Thomas attended Albert's lectures and marveled at the depth of wisdom in this man. It was exciting to discover someone who so generously proffered the treasure Thomas valued most. It was also intimidating. Thomas grew even more silent in his presence, and more studious.

When Thomas was younger, he had been called "the Ox of Sicily" by local peasants because of his impressive stature and dignified bearing as he walked past them in the fields near his home. The nickname accompanied him into adulthood, even to Paris. In the august presence of Master Albert, however, the natural reserve of the "the Ox of Sicily" was so intensified that his nickname evolved to "The Dumb Ox" by which he was known for the rest of his life.

In silence, Thomas prepared his texts, and in silence he listened to Albert's lectures. In silence he processed, organized, and developed what he learned. Rarely did he speak, except when forced by circumstances, and then he was as brief as possible. Few suspected the penetrating light his intellect brought to the material. Master Albert the Great, however, had an inkling.

After three years in Paris, Thomas was ready to begin his formal studies in theology. At that same time, Albert the Great was asked by the order to return to Germany to establish a Dominican university in Cologne where a flourishing cathedral school for younger children had been established. Much to everyone's surprise, Albert requested permission from the order for Thomas to accompany him as academic assistant.

Thomas said little, but nodded his assent when the kindly master general, John von Wildeshausen, informed him of Albert's request. His eyes alone betrayed his pleased surprise. This was an ideal situation for Thomas. He would earn his degree under the guidance of the best mentor the world had ever known. He hoped he might be of some help, both with the details of setting up the new university and with research for Albert's ongoing writing project.

Thomas knew that Albert was working on a groundbreaking project in his spare time. Albert's familiarity with Aristotle surpassed that of most scholars at that time, so his colleagues had urged him to write an exposition of Aristotle's known works, "in order to make the mind of the Greek philosopher intelligible to the Latin world," they said. Thomas, who had been reading and re-reading Aristotle since his first encounter with "the Philosopher" at Naples, was genuinely interested in the project.

Albert and Thomas took up residence at the cathedral school in Cologne in the spring of 1248, and began preparations to open a *studium* in the coming autumn. The modest four-hundred-year-old cathedral burned to the ground in late April, but by the Feast of the Assumption, August 15 of that same year, the foundation of a new and far more glorious cathedral had been laid. Its gothic spires soon pierced the sky, offering inspiration to scholars and faithful alike, directing their minds and hearts upward. The transition from cathedral school to *studium generale* was smooth. Other new Dominican *studia* in Europe were thriving, and no one doubted that this one, too, would succeed.

Once the practical details were tended to, courses began at the nascent university in earnest. Albert led a class on the work of a sixth-century Syrian author known to academia as Pseudo-Dionysius. The text he used, *On the Divine Names*, was an early philosophical consideration of what can be known by man about God, based on the names for God in Revelation. It was a challenging work. Albert lectured; Thomas took notes and pondered, without saying a word.

A fellow Dominican student noticed Thomas' silence in and out of class. He assumed the young friar was struggling with his studies. "I can help you work through some of this material," he offered. "It can be difficult at times." Thomas gratefully agreed. During their study time, the two found a quiet corner of the priory to sit down. While Thomas listened, the other student outlined the material they had gone over in class. It was not long, however, before he became confused. Thomas prompted him with the next step. Nodding his thanks, the friar resumed his explanation for a moment but soon found himself hopelessly lost in the tangle of reasoning, and became flustered.

Moved by sympathy, Thomas explained the arguments imbedded in the material to this new friend. It seemed easy and surprisingly clear the way "the Dumb Ox" said it. He filled in missing steps and highlighted the arguments with examples. The well-meaning friar soon realized how greatly he had misjudged Thomas. Thrilled with the discovery, he asked if they could meet regularly to study together so that Thomas could help *him*. Thomas readily agreed. "But please don't mention it to anyone," he asked.

The few who were aware of Thomas' quiet genius grew fond of him and filled with respect. With the enthusiasm of youth, they felt everyone should appreciate his great gifts. When another of the students came across notes that had fallen unnoticed from Thomas' books, he hurried to show them to Master Albert. Even Albert was astonished by the notes. They revealed much more than a mere class outline; they displayed profound insight and more fully developed thought than could possibly have been gleaned from a lecture.

Albert decided to put his soft-spoken prodigy to a test. He scheduled a classroom debate that would focus on a complex question they had considered in class. Albert assigned Thomas the prominent role of *respondens*. He would have to listen to a statement set forth by an opponent, and determine the logic of further assertions made by the opponent, explaining how they were consistent or inconsistent with the original claim. The opponent's role was to trip up the *respondens*, forcing him into an illogical conclusion.

On the appointed day, Thomas stood reluctantly at the front of the lecture hall that until then had seemed a reasonable size, but now seemed cavernous. The faces before him appeared countless, and their obvious expectation was intimidating in the extreme. He shifted uneasily on his feet and couldn't think what on earth to do with his hands.

Once his opponent began to speak, however, everything else in the room faded from his consciousness and his attention turned exclusively to the statement being read. His natural reticence was overcome by his acute interest in the material. When addressed, he answered easily and distinctly. He never lost the thread of reasoning or missed a logical step. He spoke with an authority that no one, not even Thomas himself, had expected. At the end of the debate, the students applauded, and Albert smiled to himself. Shedding his usual formality, Albert exclaimed, *"We call him the Dumb Ox, but he will make such a bellowing that it will echo throughout the world!"*

From that day on, Albert took Thomas' academic formation seriously into his care. He appointed the Dumb Ox a regular *respondens*, and a *cursor*, who reads Scripture and presents it to the class. As Albert's personal apprentice, he assembled material for his lectures and copied the manuscripts of his commentaries. Although Albert was a theologian, he offered philosophical tutorials as well, out of a conviction that theology must be grounded in reason. Thomas, much to his delight, was able to attend and assist with both.

The year 1250 was momentous for Thomas and for his family, and indeed for Italy. Spiritually Thomas was changed forever when, after two years in Cologne, he was ordained into the priesthood. By that momentous act at the hands of the archbishop of Cologne, he was linked through an unbroken line of succession to the original twelve apostles, the intimate friends and followers of Christ Himself. He was only twenty-five years old, the youngest age at which a Dominican could be ordained, but his superiors had no doubt that he was ready. In his daily life, filled with prayer, reading, and lecturing, he was entirely immersed in the things of God. When he addressed a congregation for the first time as a priest, he observed: "By teaching, we learn; by preaching, we are edified. If a man listens to the word of God and speaks of it in order to edify others, his own heart is changed for the better and he becomes more closely joined to God."

There was nothing Thomas longed for so much as union with God. He had been given an agile intellect hungry for truth, and that truth, he knew, was found perfectly in God. The more he beheld the order and beauty of truth, the more he longed to draw near to its Author. In the priesthood, he would be as close to God as it was possible to be in this life, a mediator between God and man in the redemptive work of Christ. Humbly he reflected that through this special office, the soul of the priest was "likened to Christ Himself."

Everyone noticed Thomas' joy. When his students commented on it, Thomas tried to illustrate for them the tremendous gift of the priesthood: "It is a special kind of bond with Christ, unlike any other. Just as a Roman coin was marked with an image of Caesar, so the soul of the priest is marked with the image of Christ. This mark not only identifies the recipient as belonging to Christ, it actually *accomplishes a likeness* in the powers of the soul, so that as a priest, he truly can bring Christ to others." That is what he longed to do, and what he was convinced he was called to do.

For the Aquino family, the year 1250 was pivotal. Since Rinaldo's execution, which they considered a martyrdom, the Aquinos lived under a cloud of fear. Would Frederick retaliate against them for what he considered Rinaldo's treachery? None of the family ventured to serve in the imperial forces or to mingle in the imperial court; yet any day the emperor might demand their presence. How would they answer him if he did, and still expect to live? Some of them, whose absence from imperial service would be especially conspicuous, took refuge in the remoteness of their fortress at Monte San Germano. The Aquinos' precarious social position not only upset their domestic serenity, but it also strained their finances severely.

In a tenuous effort to regain some of their former stability, Lady Theodora begged Pope Innocent IV to appoint her son Friar Thomas to the abbacy of Monte Cassino, now that the reigning abbot, Stephen II, was dying. "As abbot, Thomas could protect and support our family. He is determined to remain forever a Dominican," she sighed, "but perhaps that could be overlooked?"

Extraordinary as the request seemed, these were extraordinary times and Pope Innocent agreed to it. He was aware of Thomas' spiritual and intellectual aptitude, and he was sympathetic with the Aquino family's need.

Thomas, however, respectfully but emphatically declined. The honors and duties involved in such a post were not within his desires or abilities, he was certain. On the other hand, he was concerned about his family's struggles. It pained him to see his proud mother threatened with poverty, and cringing in the cruel shadow of the Emperor. With some effort, he found a charitable source of funds within the Church. Rather than forsake his life's work, he appealed to the Holy Father to be allowed to secure these funds for the aid of his family.

But the greatest relief came for the Aquinos, and to Italy, through an act of providence. In November of that same year, fifty-six-year-old Frederick Hohenstaufen grew gravely ill while *en route* to one of his garrisons in the east of Italy. He was brought by litter to a nearby hunting lodge, just south of his Mohammedan colony at Lucera. The lodge was called "Fiorentino," a name derived from the word *flora*. This small word that to most people denotes vegetation and the simple beauty of flowers, worked havoc in the soul of the larger-than-life prince.

Frederick had long believed in a prophesy that he would die in a place that took its name from the Italian word *flora*. Few people other than himself were aware of this prophesy. Throughout his life he had taken great care to avoid any place bearing a name of that origin. Whenever his campaigns brought him to the region of Tuscany, he carefully skirted its capital, Florence, for that reason.

On the fateful day that his general happened to mention the name of this lodge in which he lay, Frederick shrieked and swore and flailed in his bed. The general was startled, and the doctor who attended the emperor was greatly alarmed. It was not long, however, before Frederick subsided. With the resignation of a captured fugitive, he suddenly announced, *"This is the spot, long ago foretold to me, where I must die; the will of God be done."*

Over the next few weeks, Frederick disposed of matters of state. The empire was to pass into the hands of Conrad, his eldest living legitimate son. He divided the remainder of his realm and great wealth among his other son, Manfred, his grandson, Frederick, and his illegitimate offspring. He asked that all his debts be paid, and that "restitution be made to the Holy Roman Church."

The "Wonder of the World" requested to die in the unbleached white habit of the Cistercians, an austere branch of the Benedictine Religious order that he had always admired. He confessed his sins to the defrocked Archbishop of Palermo, and on December 13, in the year 1250, Frederick Hohenstaufen died. It was not the end of Hohenstaufen tyranny and strife in the Holy Roman Empire, nor in the life of the Aquinos, but it was a much-welcomed respite.

Chapter Six

A SCHOLASTIC TEMPEST IN A PARISIAN TEAPOT

The turbulent wind in the political sails of Italy abated for a time, but a tempest had begun to brew in the world of scholasticism. It was localized, centered at the University of Paris with waves that were potentially seismic. Into this storm, a reluctant Thomas d'Aquino was sent to lecture as a bachelor of theology in preparation for mastership. Master Albert was the driving force. He insisted that his pupil was exceptionally well prepared, both intellectually and morally.

"While it is true," he admitted, "that at age twenty-seven you are well below the minimum age for mastership, that is of far less significance than your level of understanding."

Thomas did not feel so confident; it would mean lecturing daily among peers nearly twice his age. Most bachelors at the University of Paris had spent long years publicly reading and explaining the subtleties of complex texts. He himself had only a few months of experience lecturing as a student at Cologne. Worst of all, the Dominican presence at the university was bitterly resented by the secular faculty. In particular, the professorial "chair" that Thomas was expected to assume at the culmination of his studies was hotly disputed.

The prospect before him was daunting, but Albert was determined. Moreover, Albert's influential friend, Cardinal Hugh of Saint Cher, once a master at Paris himself, was convinced Thomas was equal to the task. The Cardinal often visited Albert at Cologne and knew his prodigy well. He urged the Dominican Master General, John von Wildeshausen, to send Thomas. So, in the spring of 1252, Thomas went dutifully but apprehensively to Paris to prepare for his mastership.

The animosity at the University of Paris had its origin in the Dominican presence at that acclaimed institution for the previous thirty-five years. Almost immediately after their arrival, conflicts emerged between the ambitions of the secular powers and the religious ideals of the mendicants. The Dominicans had been sent there by Friar Dominic to study theology so that they could effectively educate others in the Catholic faith for the salvation of souls. The secular faculty at the university naturally had more interest in the practical matters that affected their careers and incomes.

When the first seven Dominicans arrived in 1217, they were welcomed by university administrators who knew they would be diligent students and would add to the institution's tenor of dignity and scholarship. The university appointed a master from among the faculty to serve as their lector at the priory of Saint-Jacques.

At first all was well. The Dominican scholars progressed from students in the liberal arts to bachelors, and quickly went on to earn the status of masters in theology. At the priory of Saint-Jacques, the number and quality of students increased at an unprecedented rate. Eventually the Dominicans made up a larger portion of the university students, secular and religious, than did the secular school of theology. The imbalance raised eyebrows among the secular faculty, who feared for their jobs.

Before long, the Dominicans acquired a "chair of theology," a position of honor and influence reserved for only the most accomplished professors. Any academic chair had an element of "hereditary right"—whoever held a chair was expected to prepare a successor. For religious, this meant another member of his order would follow in his place after he left. Thus, once a Dominican held a chair, it was understood that a Dominican would always hold that chair. When Roland of Cremona, a master of arts and "the glory of the University of Bologne," became a Dominican and moved to the priory on rue Saint-Benoit, his academic standing required that he assume the position of "chair of theology."

The Dominicans gained a second professorial chair when John of Saint Giles, who already held a master's chair at the university, joined the Dominican order. He surprised his congregation and the university officials one afternoon by taking his vows during a sermon he was preaching about the beauty of the life of religious poverty.

"My dear brethren," Master John had proclaimed on that eventful day. "In his final testament, Dominic de Guzman exhorted his followers, saying, 'O my children, my brethren, love, revere and observe Holy Poverty.' For Dominic saw with saintly vision a wonderful truth. He wrote for the benefit of his spiritual children, 'Voluntary poverty, although she may appear less comely than the other virtues outwardly, yet is the more fair and precious interiorly, well-endowed with spiritual wealth. Her merit cannot be paid with the price of this earth. And therefore, the Kingdom of Heaven is assigned as her reward.'" Master John of Saint Giles continued with fervor: "For, brethren, only when we are stripped of every possession and attachment, as was our own precious savior on Mount Calvary, are we truly free to behold for eternity the face of Him who in His lifetime sought no earthly treasure save our own hearts. 'For our sake, he became poor although he was rich, so that by his poverty we might become rich.'"

At this point in his homily, Master John descended the pulpit to receive the Dominican habit from the hand of Friar Jordan of Saxony. Robed in black and white, he then returned to the pulpit to conclude his homily. "How blessed are the poor in spirit, who by their poverty have purchased the pearl of great price. *In nomine Patris, et Filii, et Spiritus Sancti*, Amen." Thus, John of Saint Giles, master of philosophy, respected physician, and doctor of theology, had become a Dominican friar. From that day forward, two academic "chairs" belonged to the Dominicans.

Four years later yet another chairman, Alexander of Hales, entered the religious life as a Franciscan, but maintained his status on the consortium of masters. The mendicant religious were now a significant part of that representative body of professors. But their single-hearted interest was in the salvation of souls, not in the University of Paris *per se*. Their zeal contributed to their tremendous success but it also led to conflicts with the secular masters, especially regarding university politics.

The hostility between the secular and religious faculties was exacerbated when the consortium of masters organized a strike in an effort to force the city of Paris to address some of their practical concerns. The Dominicans and Franciscans were not interested in striking. "It would be unseemly for religious mendicants to attempt to force policy by political action," the teaching friars insisted. They continued to teach, and their pupils continued to study, rendering the strike ineffective. The secular faculty fumed. Of the twelve chairs in the consortium of masters, three belonged by statute to administrators, and now three more had fallen into the hands of the mendicants; the seculars were in danger of losing their political leverage at the university.

Enter William of Saint-Amour, self-appointed champion of the secular cause. Saint-Amour was a noted scholar and the presiding dean of the consortium of masters when Thomas arrived. Although Saint-Amour joined the faculty ten years after the first Dominicans, he took their presence at the esteemed university as a personal affront. In his eyes, they were a scourge upon academia and upon the world. He was determined to use his influence to eradicate the pestilence of preaching friars.

Under his deanship, the consortium of masters passed a rule that restricted each religious order to only one chair. "It is intolerable that the Dominicans have two chairs," William of Saint-Amour expostulated within the consortium. "The second one, at the very least, should not be allowed."

Unfortunately for Thomas, he was being sent to Paris to fill that second, disputed chair.

The administration at the university had countermanded William of Saint-Amour's hostile regulation, but he and his collaborators on the faculty were adamant nevertheless. They drew up a document, in league with a local bishop, excommunicating the mendicants until they agreed to cooperate with all of the new statutes, and strictly limiting each religious order to only one professorial chair.

For the sake of peace, the Dominicans tried to accept the demands of the vociferous seculars. But Pope Innocent IV, whom they were sworn to obey, overruled the edict of excommunication against them and insisted that they maintain their *status quo* at the university, including the two Dominican chairs. Under a dark cloud of secular disapprobation, the youthful Thomas d'Aquino commenced his studies for the disputed Dominican chair of theology.

In the fall of 1252, Thomas could do nothing to alleviate the situation. He was utterly powerless, so he simply went about his appointed work. He would be lecturing as a *Sententiarius*, treating the theological questions addressed by Peter Lombard in his glossary of early Christian sources. He gave his full attention to class preparations. Within a few weeks, the results were apparent. Other masters at the university noticed that his teaching was making an impression on the students. "I have heard that his teaching is somehow different," wrote Elias Brunet, the Dominican master who held the chair for foreigners at that time. He was reporting to Cardinal Hugh of Saint Cher. "His students say it all seems so novel—new arrangements, new methods of proof, new arguments. It is as if his mind were full of a new light."

The clarity with which Thomas taught was unusual in a bachelor, and his ability to illustrate with fresh and fitting analogies added to the effectiveness of his lectures. His prodigious memory allowed him to connect diverse passages of Scripture, to bring out their meaning and highlight them with the observations and arguments of pagan philosophers and Christian thinkers. He made profound concepts easy to grasp. In his hands, the truth seemed both rich and accessible.

The text he taught from, *The Sentences* of Peter Lombard, was a part of the fiber of his mind. He had memorized it while captive at Roccasecca, and had since given it a great deal of thought. In four volumes, it treated the doctrines of Christianity in the order of the Trinitarian Creed, beginning with what is known about God as Father, and then as Son, and finally as the Holy Spirit. Thomas remained entirely faithful to this Trinitarian formula, but he emphasized a new order for teaching the doctrines that his students found illuminating. First and foremost, he focused on the Oneness of God and then he divided the rest of the doctrines into those that flow from God and those that lead creatures back to God, who is the ultimate end of His creation.

While Thomas and his Dominican brothers studied and taught, William of Saint-Amour preached sermons against them, mocked them publicly and in writing, and criticized their way of life. "The mendicants are using their vows as an excuse to live off the hard work of others. 'Poverty' as they practice it, cannot be a legitimate way of life." He contended that it was immoral for the mendicants to depend on others for their livelihood. They should support themselves by manual labor, he said, and restrict themselves to a life of prayer. He was determined that they did not belong in academia.

In an effort to gain the support of the highest ecclesial authority, Saint-Amour composed an outline of his grievances against the mendicant orders. In his tract, he quoted the prophetic words of Saint Paul calling the last days "dangerous times in which men shall have an appearance of godliness, but denying the power thereof," claiming that this had been an early warning of the era of mendicant religious. He sent it to Pope Innocent IV, along with a blatantly heretical tract written by a Franciscan friar, Gerard de Borgo San Donnino, as proof of the insidious threat of the mendicants.

"The age of the Eternal Gospel is upon us," the fanatical Franciscan, Donnino, had written. "The church of Christ with its laws and sacraments is in its final epoch. The Franciscans are the army of the new age destined to overthrow the reigning order! Behold their numbers grow." It was all the evidence Saint-Amour needed. He was confident that Donnino's extremism, paired with his own articulate objections, would open the eyes of the pope to the evil of begging friars. Next, Saint-Amour turned all his efforts to inciting antagonistic public opinion against the friars in Paris.

"Mendici non debent praedicere! Praedicatores non debent orare!" "Beggars don't preach! Preachers don't beg!" shouted a mob of angry students outside the priory of Saint-Jacques. "Saint-Amour's henchmen," said Friar John of Saint Giles and shook his head and grumbled as he hurried through the gates of the priory, dodging flying pellets of rock and mud.

"Attention! *Il est l'antechrist!* There is the antichrist!" taunted a Parisian youth. "Antichrist! Antichrist!" echoed a chorus of childish voices. A volley of mud flew past the wrought iron gate, spattering the Friar's white scapular. A clutch of street urchins tittered and ran away with the telltale mud dripping from their hands.

"I suppose this is a good sign," observed another friar who had been watching from the courtyard. "After all, 'What servant is greater than his master?'" he quoted the Scriptures as he helped Friar John wipe off his habit. "It is as Our Lord promised, 'As they persecuted me, so they will they persecute you.'"

"I wish I were more like Our Lord and could readily turn the other cheek," Friar John muttered. "I used to excel at *calcio*; how I long to hone my kicking skills on the seat of their trousers."

The second friar looked a little startled. "I am sorry," Friar John chuckled. "It was a harrowing walk from the university. The mobs are growing bold, and their hatred is as thick as the mud they sling."

Much to the delight of William of Saint-Amour and his cohorts, after only a few months of deliberation, Pope Innocent issued a surprising precautionary edict banning the Dominicans and Franciscans from preaching and hearing confessions without explicit permission from their local bishops. It was a small victory, but it reinforced the antipathy of Saint-Amour and his companions and added force to their anti-mendicant propaganda. The tract by Donnino, the fanatic Franciscan, was condemned as heretical and publicly burned.

Within two months, however, Pope Innocent IV died and was replaced as Vicar of Christ by Pope Alexander IV. This aged pontiff was a friend and protector of the early Franciscans, and more familiar with their aims and inner workings. He had overseen the canonization of Saint Clare of Assisi, and verified the claim that Saint Francis of Assisi had received the stigmata, the wounds of Christ in his hands and feet. As head of the Church, Pope Alexander rescinded the previous pope's ban and restored the order's former privileges.

William of Saint-Amour did not concede defeat. He multiplied his efforts to defame the mendicants, using every opportunity to ridicule and criticize them. All but a handful of secular masters began to distance themselves from Saint-Amour. His students, on the other hand, became so incensed that the king of France set his royal guards outside the priory gates to protect the friars from the mobs.

During that spring of 1256, Thomas received his license to become a master in theology. This required that he offer a public lecture for all the masters at the university, followed by two days of talks and debates. At the culmination of the process, if all went well, he would be awarded his mastership and admitted to the consortium of masters to fill the second, and highly controversial, Dominican chair.

As the time for his inception drew near, he became extremely reluctant and begged to be exempted. He was still below the canonical age of thirty-five, and he felt he was not yet adequately prepared to be a master. He would prefer to continue as a bachelor, and avoid adding fuel to the heated controversy. This request was firmly declined; he must incept as a master immediately. The chancellor of the university, his own academic master, Elias Brunet, his Dominican superior, Humbert of Romans, and, in fact, the pope himself—by letter—insisted that he was ready, and was the best candidate to incept.

Thomas prayed for a way out of the situation. He knew that his presence would incite the indignation of the more seasoned, the more accomplished—and the more irascible—masters on the faculty. In anguish he prayed for deliverance at night in his room. Many years later, he told his prior that as he slept one night during this troubling time, he experienced a vivid dream, almost a vision.

He dreamed that a kindly old man whom he believed to be Saint Dominic approached him. The man asked what was troubling the young Dominican. Thomas told him he did not feel worthy to take up the position of master, and he did not know what he could possibly speak about in the inaugural lecture. The gentle man in his dream assured him that God would provide the strength and wisdom to perform his duties as master well. For the lecture, he told Thomas to speak about the Psalm that says, '*From your heights you water the mountains, the earth is filled with the fruits of your works.*'

The first day set aside for his inception at last arrived. The required "disputes," formal debates on connected theological questions, went smoothly enough. It was now time for the *principium*, the inaugural lecture. Thomas stood at the front of the room and looked out at the assembled faculty: senior masters, junior masters, interested bachelors and students of the arts, even the university chancellor. All eyes regarded the giant young Dominican, the Dumb Ox, as he took a deep breath and began, "'*Rigans montes de superioribus suis; de fructu operum tuorum satisabitur terra…*' From the heights you water the mountains, the earth is filled with the fruits of your works, declares Psalm 103."

In the attentive stillness of the lecture hall, Thomas unfolded this passage of Scripture. "Rain falls from the heavens, the mountains receive its richness, and the rivers of water pour down into the fertile valleys below," he said. "Similarly, from the heights of divine wisdom the minds of the learned, represented by the mountains, are watered by whose ministry the light of divine wisdom reached to the minds of those who listen. God is the giver of all that is good, all wisdom comes from Him." He iterated the ways that God's wisdom is "like the rain in its sublimity," and that teachers are like the lofty mountains refreshed by rain and illumined by the sun, providing protection from ignorance. To be effective, he went on, they must be upright like the mountains, elevated in truth and virtue. The learner is like the earth in the valley below, fertile, humble and firm in judgment. "There is an order in the communication of wisdom that reflects the order found in nature."

He used analogies from the natural world and from common experience, along with passages from the Old and the New Testament. In conclusion, he outlined the preeminent virtues of a wise teacher, and recalled that without God we can do nothing,

"'But although no one by himself, of himself, is sufficient for such a ministry, he can hope to have this sufficiency from God'; 2 Corinthians 3:5: 'Not that we are sufficient of ourselves to think anything, as from ourselves, but our sufficiency is from God.' He must ask it of God; James 1:5: 'But if any of you is wanting in wisdom, let him ask it of God, who gives abundantly to all men, and does not reproach; and it will be given to him.'"

His objectors were silent; his supporters, confirmed. Thomas was awarded the doctor's cap and signet ring. He was now eligible to occupy the second Dominican chair.

The consortium of masters, however, refused to admit him. William of Saint-Amour threatened to call a strike and demand that the faculty and students leave the city in protest, not of Thomas in particular, he said, but of any Dominican in their consortium.

At just that time, Saint-Amour released a second tract, *The Perils of the Last Times*, condemning the mendicants as the Anti-Christ, complete with theological arguments and an array of prophesies. It was distributed to all the bishops of France in the hope that they would take action to crush the mendicants. The king of France, Louis IX, gave it little credence, but because of its incendiary effect, he sent it to the pope for judgment. King Louis himself greatly admired the mendicants and wanted the issue settled. The pope appointed a commission of three cardinals to examine the text.

While the papal theologians studied the merits of Saint-Amour's written attack, Thomas and a prominent Franciscan friend at the university, Friar Bonaventure, considered how best to address the problematic situation. Bonaventure and Thomas had a sympathy of conviction. Both were devoted to the life of poverty and prayer. And they were united in the belief that the love of truth was a path to God. They studied and taught so that others could travel that same path. The honor of official acceptance into the consortium of masters, or the denial of that honor, held little significance for either of them. Unfortunately, however, their students could not receive academic recognition for attending their classes without that academic nod. For the sake of the students, the situation had to be resolved.

Bonaventure had come to Paris as a young Friar Minor in 1242, and had received his licentiate to teach three years prior to Thomas. In 1256, the consortium of masters still refused to accept him, and he finally gave up lecturing because of the violence of the protests that erupted around him. That summer both Thomas and Bonaventure composed careful rebuttals to Saint-Amour's most recent attack, and presented the to the pope's panel of theologians residing at the ancient walled city of Anagni. Albert the Great, who was now the provincial of the German Dominicans, made the long trek to Anagni to offer his support.

Bonaventure's essay, *On the Poverty of Christ*, gave a moving defense of the religious vow of total poverty as an imitation of the poverty of Christ. Thomas' treatise, *Against the Accusers*, served as a theological justification of the role of mendicants in Christianity. Beginning with the words of the Psalms, "'Lo, your enemies have made a noise: and those who hate you have lifted up the head.' *They have taken malicious counsel against your people*." Thomas noted the obvious ill will of the accusers but painstakingly addressed their claims. With charity and earnestness, and with some humor directed at the more absurd accusations made by the detractors, he clarified the charges Saint-Amour made against the religious orders, and then addressed them one by one.

On October 5 of that year, word reached Paris that the Chair of Peter had decided in favor of the mendicants. Saint-Amour's text was refuted and condemned.

Its unrepentant author was soon exiled by the King of France to his rural native village of Saint-Amour in the Maconnais district of Burgundy, two hundred miles away. His colleagues at the university were forced to apologize publicly for undue belligerence. Both Thomas and Bonaventure were at last admitted to the consortium of masters. Later it would become evident that a hot wind can still agitate the waters from two hundred miles away, but for the present, controversy at Paris subsided and relative peace was restored.

Chapter Seven

THE EYE OF THE STORM

"Out of one storm, into another," Thomas laughed to himself. He and his companions pulled up the hems of their black *cappas*, heavy with rain, river, and mud, as they dragged their boat out of the water and onto the Alpine shore. The agitated river had proved too strong for their weary hired rowers, so Thomas suggested that he and his traveling companions offer assistance.

With unusual agility for a man of such bulk, he leapt over the side. He was followed somewhat less enthusiastically by his confreres. Together they gripped the line, pulling against the current. The three black-and-white-clad friars dragged the boat and its surprised oarsmen to shore. They were making their way from Paris to Naples through the unpredictable climate of the Alps.

Thomas glanced upward as a bolt of lightning charged the sky, illuminating the landscape with its eerie gray-green light. He made a sign of the cross, uttering almost mechanically, "God came in the flesh, God suffered for us." He did not like thunderstorms. The friars had long miles ahead of them and could not allow a mere cloudburst to slow them down.

Near the end of the academic year 1259, Thomas, now age thirty-four, was summoned to the general chapter of Dominicans in Valenciennes, northeast of Paris. There he had joined a commission of scholars including Albert and a few other renowned masters from Paris. Their task was to establish rules for the ongoing intellectual formation of the order. Consistent with the ideals of their order's founder, each of them shared the conviction that young preachers require a solid academic background for their own sake and for the sake of their teaching apostolate. Together they established policies to ensure that every Dominican be well formed, and that his studies never cease. Learning is a lifelong process, they insisted; for it nourishes the soul.

After the chapter meeting that spring, Thomas and the new presiding master general, Humbert of Romans, returned to Paris. By the end of June, one of Thomas' students, William of Alton, was prepared to succeed Thomas on the consortium of masters in the Dominican chair for foreigners. Thomas presided over his inception, and was then free to return to the Roman Province and his home priory of San Domenico in Naples.

Bound by the vow of poverty, Friar Thomas, Friar Humbert, and a younger Dominican student, Friar Conrad of Sessa, traveled the one thousand miles from Paris to Naples on foot. They walked, day after day, through chill and heat, rain, fog, and sunshine, stopping once daily under the open sky to eat whatever they had been able to beg or buy from local peasants and fellow travelers. Sometimes they had enough to share with the ubiquitous Alpine marmots that tentatively approached the friars when they sat down to eat. Sometimes they would satisfy themselves with prayer and the confidence that God will provide, rather than with actual food if there were none to be had.

By night, they slept beneath the stars or in haylofts, wrapped in their versatile *cappas* for comfort and warmth. By day, they skirted the rocky slopes of the Alps that were dotted with yellow wormwood and blue chicory. Adorning the steep rocky ledges were sprays of delicate pink rock-jasmine that put the friars in mind of the working of God's grace, insinuating its roots and gently eroding the stony hardness of the human heart.

The blue of the summer sky on fair days paled against the deeper blue and stark white of the high distant peaks—it looked to the friars that nothing but thin mountain air lay between the Alps and heaven itself. Against a background of chirping crickets, cooing rock pigeons, and the carefree song of crag martins, they prayed the Divine Office, recited the rosary, and debated theological questions. They spoke, too, of family matters and issues of state.

The Alpine route was an artery for European travel. Rarely were the three friars entirely alone for a whole day. On the path through the Alps they encountered a cross-section of medieval humanity: pilgrims on their way to Rome, statesmen and their retinues, religious *en route* to chapter meetings, students and professors making the way to larger universities on either side of the Alps. The strangers exchanged pleasantries, along with political opinions, and news of the war now raging in the papal states under the beleaguered Pope Alexander IV. Italian political machinations were a favorite topic of conversation among the wayfarers.

After the death of Emperor Frederick II, his son, Conrad Hohenstaufen, took the helm of state. But the son never broke loose from his father's wake to take control of Italy. Only four years into his reign, he succumbed to malaria. The country then splintered into factions of Guelfs and Ghibellines, while demi-rulers emerged right and left. The Guelfs were staunch supporters of papal authority in a free national state. Ghibellines sought to raise an empire, oppressive or not, with Italy at its head.

It did not take long for Manfred—illegitimate offspring of the "Wonder of the World"—to rise above the fray. Manfred was like his father in many ways, but lacked redeeming greatness. He had stolen the crown of Sicily from his infant nephew, Conradin, Conrad's legitimate heir, and began to force himself on the rest of Italy, gradually expanding the boundaries of the Two Sicilies.

While the uncle was maneuvering to rule the Roman world, the child heir, Conradin, wielded his silver spoon only over the Duchy of Swabia in Germany where the Hohenstaufen family originated. A miniscule kingdom for a miniscule king, it was the source of jests. Pope Alexander IV, however, was much too weary to be amused. He determined to put an end, once and for all, to the outrageous Hohenstaufen abuse of power. Wherever their sympathies lay, the broad range of Alpine travelers whom the monks encountered agreed on one thing: Italy was in disarray.

By late autumn, the three friars had reached their destinations. Humbert of Romans arrived in Rome in time to preside over the provincial chapter there, and the other two friars proceeded on to the priory of San Domenico in Naples. Thomas immediately assumed the duties of lector for the priory where sixteen years before he had taken the habit under the shadow of his mother's disapprobation.

His proud mother had suffered a great deal since then. After the loss of her two sons, at least one of whom she considered a martyr, she had let the servants go and had taken what remained of her household away from Roccasecca, hoping for the security of anonymity.

But as she neared the end of her life, she was now content in the loving and capable hands of her daughters, Adalasia, Theodora, and Mary, all of whom had married well. Her eldest son, Aimo, a tribute to her proud family heritage, was a count in his own right and a preeminent knight in service to the pope. Her eldest daughter, Marrotta, had passed away after a short but exemplary life as the abbess of the Benedictine convent of Saint Mary in Capua. Theodora's husband, Roger of San Severino, Count of Marsico, was something of a hero in the family. He had served with Rinaldo in the conspiracy against Frederick and had escaped from the imperial siege of Cappacio. Now he and his wife lived in that noble family's castle near the Tyrrhenian Sea, southeast of Naples.

And then there was Thomas. He was not perhaps all she had hoped, but she thought he was a good young man; he seemed to endear himself to all who encountered him. He was startlingly absent-minded for an Aquino but she understood that he was well respected in some circles at least. She could still hold her head up. She was sanguine, too, that the tyranny of the Hohenstaufen's was soon to end and the rising generation of the Aquino family would regain stature in Italy. Manfred was weak, and Conradin weaker still. The pope was making overtures to foreign kings for aid. Perhaps they would find a way to restore peace. There was hope. There was always hope.

As he delivered the morning's lecture one day at the priory that autumn, Thomas articulated the rational basis of Christian hope. He looked out thoughtfully at a room filled with Dominicans, young men and old. "In the words of Jeremiah, God speaks to us," he said. "*'I know the plans I have for you,' says the Lord, 'plans for your welfare and not for harm, to give you a future with hope. Then when you call upon me and come and pray to me, I will hear you. When you search for me, you will find me; if you seek me with all your heart, I will let you find me', says the Lord'."*

Calm conviction permeated his words. "Saint Paul tells us in his letter to the Romans, 'we are saved by hope.' Yet in the letter to the Ephesians he says that through grace 'we are saved by faith.' Of course, both statements are true, one as a consequence of the other. For in faith we know that we are loved by God, as Saint John says—*'In this is charity: not as though we had loved God, but because He hath first loved us.'* And through that gift of faith, we rest secure in the love of God."

The first pale rays of morning light crept into the hushed room as Thomas continued. "Recall from Aristotle's *Ethics* that a person is loved in himself when the lover wishes the good for him, even if the lover may receive nothing from him. Now since there is produced in man, by sanctifying grace, an act of loving God for Himself, the result is that man obtains hope from God by means of grace. For when one person loves another, and knows that he is loved by that other, he must get hope from him. It follows, then, that from the same gift of grace from which flows faith, one obtains hope."

As the hall emptied at the close of the lecture, Thomas turned to Friar Reginald beside him. "It is hope that the followers of Mohammed lack, Reginald, hope in the possibility of friendship with God. Their philosophers have led them astray. And it is hope that we must strive to offer them, so far as it lies within our abilities."

Friar Reginald of Piperno was Thomas' newly appointed *socius*, a secretary assigned by the Dominican order to help Thomas with the practical details of his work. Every Dominican teaching master was given a *socius*. Reginald nodded his concurrence, and mentally prepared himself for hours of dictation. For when Thomas referred to the followers of Mohammed, he was thinking of his new apologetical work, the *Summa Contra Gentiles*.

Thomas was preparing this exposition of the faith as a gift for his missionary friend, Raymond of Penyafort. The dynamic Friar Raymond had established what he called a *studium arabicum* in Barcelona. To his fellow Dominicans he often spoke of the "thick atmosphere of darkness" that he had encountered in regions of Spain and North Africa. When he spoke, his great desire to share the light of truth with the people there was almost palpable. Many, he said, misunderstood it, or had never even heard of it; but everywhere he went he found an immense hunger for truth. To combat the darkness, he needed a light by which his own missionaries could see and understand their faith. He wanted them to be clear about what could be known by reason alone, and matters of faith that could not be proved but could still be shown to be reasonable.

Thomas took this project to heart. He had once confided to Friar Reginald that he believed the chief duty of his own life was summed up in the words of Saint Hilary, that his "every word and sense might speak of God." Composing the *Summa Contra Gentiles* provided an opportunity to exercise that duty. It was edifying work, too, and confirmed for Thomas that above all human pursuits, the pursuit of wisdom is more perfect than any other because it is more noble, more useful, and, he had long-since discovered, more joyful. With the help of his faithful secretary, Thomas gave every free moment he had to the task.

Over time, the *Summa Contra Gentiles* grew into a profound reflection on the whole of theology. In four volumes, Thomas addressed the question he had asked so long ago of his father, his sisters, his teachers at Monte Cassino, and anyone else who would listen: "What is God?" He wrote about the existence of an omnipotent, intelligent, and self-subsisting being called God, beginning with what can be known about Him by sense and natural reason. He also spoke of the triune God of undying love who can be discovered by reason, beginning from revealed principles. He spoke of the creation of the world and its creatures, who proceed from His goodness and who by their very nature seek to return to Him. He unfolded the magnanimous gift of God the Son, who made it possible for creature souls to return to the creator. He treated the problems of suffering and of evil, and the purpose and order in nature, and the meaning of life after death.

As he paced the ground late into the night, dictating arguments, illustrations and commentary to Friar Reginald, his mind moved rapidly, recalling and connecting ideas he had read in pagan and Christian philosophy, in Scripture, and in the early church fathers. As he worked out his arguments, he became so entirely absorbed in his thoughts that at times the *socius* had to set down his own pen and remove the candle gently from Thomas's grip. More than once before it had burned all the way down, until the hot wax seared the master's hand unheeded.

For nearly a year in 1260, Thomas worked in Naples in relative calm. He was appointed preacher general for Naples that year, which gave him a voice in the Dominican chapter meetings, and the responsibility to preach, or provide a preacher, wherever needed throughout his region. That same year, his mother died suddenly—quitting the earth decisively, just the way she had lived. By that time, she had an inkling that her youngest son—however absent-minded—might yet be a credit to the name of Aquino, shedding light on a world in confusion.

Chapter Eight

THE EAGLE SOARS

The future held a promise of hope for the Lady Theodora d'Aquino in her final days, but Pope Alexander IV was not as sanguine in his. He lay on his deathbed at Viterbo the next year, 1261, utterly demoralized by the state of the world that had been in his charge for seven years.

Despite all of the pontiff's efforts, his power had been usurped by Manfred Hohenstaufen under his spurious claim to the crown of Sicily. He was gaining momentum in Lombardy and Tuscany. Since disloyal magistrates in Rome had formed an alliance with the illegitimate heir to the Hohenstaufen empire, the dying pope was no longer safe even in his own See.

At the University of Paris, the beacon of higher learning within Pope Alexander's jurisdiction, there was a growing antagonism to the teaching Magisterium. How easily the consortium of teaching masters disregarded his advice and warnings—at home and abroad, the pope's authority was challenged. The clergy of England had grown bitterly resentful of the papacy, especially when its politics required their financial backing. In central Europe, the Tartars were on the move and all of Alexander's attempts to unite Christians against that barbarian threat had proved futile.

Fifty years earlier, Alexander's predecessor on the papal throne, Innocent III, had received a vision of a tottering church held up by one small man in rags. That vision seemed to Alexander to have been prophetic of the time in which he lived; the Church was crumbling at last. He clung to Christ's promise that, "The gates of hell would not prevail against it," yet it was difficult for this Vicar of Christ to imagine how it would be restored. Would the growing legions of mendicants who followed in the footsteps of "The Poor Man of Assisi" really be strong enough to secure its foundations, as Pope Innocent's vision seemed to suggest? When Pope Alexander IV left the world, his only sure hope was in the mercy of God.

Within a few months of Alexander's death, an intrepid Pope Urban IV assumed the Chair of Peter and took in hand the affairs of Church and state. He, too, looked hopefully to the burgeoning orders of religious mendicants. With his approbation, all available Dominican leaders met that year in the picturesque central Italian town of Orvieto.

Built atop a bluff of volcanic stone one thousand feet high, it overlooked miles of cypress-lined Umbrian plains in every direction, an ideal setting in which to contemplate heaven and the immensity of the world in need.

As preacher general, Thomas traveled the two hundred miles from Naples to attend the chapter meeting in that city, and there he was directed by his order to remain. The newly constructed priory of San Domenico in Orvieto required a lector, and the Holy Father wanted a spiritual advisor and theologian-in-residence.

Thomas' duties as lector there coincided well with his work on the *Summa Contra Gentiles*. The material treated in his writing was the basis of a complete theological formation, providing ample matter for his lectures. The Dominican superiors were confident that the students at the priory in Orvieto would be well instructed.

At about the same time, Urban IV took up residence in Orvieto, along with the papal curia and all his court. Far removed from the quiet retirement Thomas had known at the priory in Naples, Orvieto became a bustling center of activity under Pope Urban.

"This pope will do as he wills!" predicted a Sienese ambassador one afternoon as he stood beside Thomas outside San Domenico. Pope Urban had just presided at the consecration of that first Dominican church in Orvieto. Dignitaries and religious gathered for the ceremony and celebration that followed. "I have known Pantaleon for years," the diplomat confided to Thomas. "In every capacity that he has assumed, it is the same. Rarely has any shepherd of souls been as energetic in word and deed as this man. He does everything himself!"

Thomas soon learned the accuracy of this description. Urban had inherited a leading role in a world divided and he was going to do everything in his power to unite it.

Urban IV was once simply Jacques Pantaleon, son of a French cobbler. He was deeply religious and an able statesman, a rare combination. A practical man who did not hesitate to do what he saw must be done, spiritually and politically, he advocated for the good of the souls and of the state in his care. Throughout the country, violence was erupting between bitterly divided groups. He would play his part to restore peace.

The new pope tried at first to establish a compromise with Manfred Hohenstaufen, but that proved fruitless. Next, he turned with faint hope to the adolescent Conradin Hohenstaufen, Duke of Swabia, legitimate heir of the Hohenstaufen dynasty. Perhaps, Urban thought, with a great deal of guidance, Conradin would be able to stem Manfred's advance. That hope, too, quickly faded when Conradin's guardian and uncle, Louis II, Duke of Upper Bavaria, adamantly refused to allow it. "The boy is young and untried," he said. "The risk to him and to the crown is far too great. We will bide our time."

Finally, Urban IV formed a cautious alliance with Charles of Anjou, the less benign brother of beloved King Louis IX of France. After several years of negotiations, Charles agreed to come to the aid of Italy.

The violence within the boundaries of Italy was an urgent concern, but the widening rift that severed Christianity into East and West also weighed heavily upon the pontiff. Because he had served as Patriarch of Jerusalem before becoming pope, he knew the sources of dissent, and where possibilities lay for concord. The Greek Emperor, Michael VIII Palaeologus, was also eager for a reunion of the Church in the East and the West. It seemed a realistic goal, and one Pope Urban IV held dear.

As a result, the papal court at Orvieto became a center of not only political and ecclesial activity, but of scholarship as well. Philosophers, theologians, poets, and linguists met and collaborated alongside ambassadors, statesmen, and generals. The Flemish Dominican, William of Moerbeke, was a prolific translator of Greek whose work Urban encouraged. The Holy Father hoped that by means of accurate translations, a better understanding of Greek thought might serve to bridge the gap between the East and the Latin West. Albert the Great had just resigned from his office as Bishop of Ratisbon in order to return to a more contemplative life, and was now free to join Thomas at Orvieto. The two worked together once again on his ongoing commentaries on the Aristotelian treatises, many of which Moerbeke had translated.

With all these forces at work in his own household, and with the help of Thomas d'Aquino's incisive mind, Urban sought ways to bring healing to the ailing world. "For the Church is the Body of Christ," he often repeated. "Scripture has foretold—and for us in our sacred office, it has commanded—'Not a bone of His body shall be broken.'"

Under Urban's patronage, Friar Moerbeke translated into Latin, for the first time, documents from the early Church councils, the First Council of Constantinople, the Council of Ephesus, and the Council of Chalcedon. Along with these, he translated writings of the early Greek fathers of the Church, men who followed in the immediate footsteps of the apostles and their first successors.

Urban requested that Thomas use these valuable transcripts to determine and explain the consistent teachings of the Church from its very roots, the earliest days of Christianity. Here was fresh hope that the conflicting views of the East and the West concerning the doctrines of processions within the Triune God, and the primacy of the See of Peter, might be resolved. These were issues of dissent in the East. If Aquinas could make them clear enough, East and West might be united once again.

Thomas pored over these new documents and gleaned from them what he needed to devise a clear philosophical account of the doctrines that divided the Church. His treatise, written in the service of this cause, was given a name: *Contra Errores Graecorum*.

At the same time, Urban IV looked for help from his scholars-in-residence to understand and address the growing turbulence at the University of Paris. A number of masters there were teaching the philosophy of Averroes, claiming it was the direct and logical consequence of the philosophy of Aristotle. It was the same confusion that had concerned earlier popes because it directly contradicted both reason and faith. Urban was considering another ban against the books of Aristotle, at least until the intellectual knot could be unraveled.

Thomas and Albert the Great hoped to deflect that extreme measure. Both men urged William of Moerbeke to work quickly to complete accurate translations of more of Aristotle's works, so that scholars would no longer be dependent on Averroes' faulty interpretations. In the meantime, Thomas continued his work on the *Summa Contra Gentiles*, where he addressed the errors of Averroes, and clarified many of the issues that agitated Paris.

Thomas and Urban IV became good friends during the years at Orvieto. They were different from each other in every accident of birth and breeding, but they were entirely one in conviction. Each in his own domain strove for unity among Christians. Both appreciated the power of truth, especially the truth of the faith they shared. And at the heart of their faith pulsated a profound love of Christ in the Sacrament of the Eucharist, the precious gift of God's presence among the people he died to save. The significance of a sacrament that was not merely a symbol of unity and love, but which contained the author of love Himself, united these two men in awe and in ardor.

In their time at Orvieto, Thomas Aquinas and Pope Urban IV both endeavored to offer an accounting of the teachings of the Church that would foster healing and unity. Preeminent was the doctrine of the Eucharist.

"At the institution of this Sacrament," Pope Urban IV wrote in an open letter to the Catholic faithful of 1264, and of all times, "Our Lord Himself said to the apostles, 'Do this in memory of me.' For us the outstanding memorial of His love would be this venerable Sacrament, a memorial in which we attain the corporeal presence of the Savior Himself. Other things which we remember we embrace spiritually and mentally; we do not thereby obtain their real presence. However, in this sacramental commemoration, Jesus Christ gave Himself as nourishment."

At the same time, Thomas wrote about the Eucharist in his *Summa Contra Gentiles*. He clarified the Catholic understanding of that sacrament for believer and unbeliever alike, emphasizing its reasonableness. Rightly understood, he hoped it would lead people to the peace found perfectly in the mystical body of Christ, the church.

"The mystery of the incarnate Word is joined to us in one way in baptism which is a spiritual rebirth, and in another way in this sacrament of the Eucharist which is a spiritual nourishment," he wrote. "In baptism, the Word incarnate is contained in his power only, but in the sacrament of the Eucharist He is contained in His substance."

Thomas explained philosophically what takes place at the moment of transubstantiation when the priest repeats the words, "This is my body." It had been understood since the time that Christ first spoke those words at the Last Supper, that when they are repeated by his consecrated successors, the host in the hands of the priest ceases to be bread and becomes the body of Christ. "This, to be sure, nature cannot do," Thomas wrote. "For every operation of nature presupposes matter which individuates substance. But matter is subject to the divine power, since the latter brings it into being. Hence, by divine power it can come about that this individual substance be converted into that pre-existing substance. What persists is other than the substance of bread; it is the substance of the body, blood, soul, and divinity of Christ. Although the substance of bread does not persist, the sensible signs of bread remain."

For the faithful, the reasoning of the theologian enriched their understanding. For the apologist, it provided a defensible account. For the theologian, it supplied the philosophical structure upon which to build the edifice of faith. For the shepherd of the Church, it was invaluable.

The pope and the theologian were not alone in their devotion to this sacrament. The Christian world at that time was alive to the real presence of Christ in the Eucharistic. With city-wide feasts and public devotions, towns throughout Europe honored the Blessed Sacrament that they fully accepted as the Body of Christ. When a priest in nearby Bolsena witnessed the host he had consecrated at Mass seeping with blood that he understood to be the blood of Christ, the entire population of that small lake town walked fifteen miles in procession to the papal palace at Orvieto to announce the miracle to the pope.

This event was a catalyst for Urban IV. As shepherd of the Church, he declared a universal feast to honor God in the Blessed Sacrament: *Corpus Christi*—the Feast of the Body and Blood of Christ.

Urban asked Thomas to compose the liturgy for the feast to express the profundity of the sacrament and the infinite love of God it implied. The pope was relying on a creativity that he suspected lay within Thomas' abilities, but that had not yet been exercised.

When the day of the newly proclaimed Feast of Corpus Christi arrived, thousands gathered at Orvieto, spilling out the doors of the cathedral into the piazza, and across the plateau. Standing before his immense congregation, the Holy Father read aloud, "Let the hearts and mouths of all break forth in hymns of saving joy. Then let faith sing, hope dance, charity exult, devotion applaud, the choir be jubilant, and purity delight! Then let each one with willing spirit and prompt will come together, laudably fulfilling his duties, celebrating the Solemnity of so great a Feast."

From within the frescoed walls of the church, strains of Thomas' *Adoro Te Devote*, resplendent poetry put into song, issued forth and echoed into the valley below:

> *Adoro te devote, latens Deitas…*
> *Godhead here in hiding, Whom I do adore,*
> *Masked by these bare shadows, Shape and nothing more,*
> *See, Lord, at Thy service, Low lies here a heart*
> *Lost, all lost in wonder*
> *At the God thou art*
> *What God's Son hath told me*
> *Take for truth I do*
> *Truth Himself speaks truly, Or there's nothing true.*

The beauty of the hymns and the poetry of the prayers that day were the reflections of a quiet heart steeped in gratitude, awe, and love. The hearts of all who heard it joined his in its upward flight.

But the serenity that enveloped the faithful that summer was soon shattered by the harsh realities of war. Pope Urban IV had been forced to flee only a few months later when a plot against his life was discovered. He was visited late one night by a courier who had been sent by his old friend, the Sienese ambassador, to warn him of the danger. The courier urged him to leave that very night.

"Your life is not secure, Your Holiness," he said. "My master has become aware of a bloody intrigue among your enemies in Siena. They intend to act at once."

The pope did not leave immediately. He spent the night in prayer, ready to meet death if it should come to that. In the morning, however, his advisors urged him to leave. He could shepherd his flock in another city, they said, and his life was vital to the unity of the church. With sadness, Pope Urban IV agreed to leave Orvieto. That was on September 9, 1264. By October 2, Pope Urban IV lay dead in Perugia, fifty miles from his palace, with his realm still deeply divided.

Papal forces had recently been defeated near the Aquino fortress at Monte San Giovanni, despite the united efforts of Aimo d'Aquino, and his uncle, Thomas II, Count of Acera. This territory was within the patrimony, the papal lands, and at the pope's request, the Aquinos had stood off the imperial onslaught for a time, but they were far outnumbered.

Manfred was expanding his grasp and gaining momentum throughout Italy. The Church of the East and the West was a house divided, and Manfred was turning his eye greedily to the East. The country was in strife, the academic world teemed with dissension, and although the 'Body of Christ' was not broken, it suffered from its wounds.

Despite three years under Urban IV's determined leadership, the world was fractured. Yet because of his efforts, the machinery was in place to produce peace as his successor, Clement IV, ascended the papal throne. Prince Charles of Anjou had finally gathered his troops and stood ready to march into Italy against Manfred's Saracen armies. Negotiations between the Church in the East and the West were underway and the treatise Thomas had written at the request of Urban IV clarified the issues that divided it.

The commentaries by Thomas and Albert on the Moerbeke translations of Aristotle began to unravel the intellectual knot that had held academia in a stranglehold. Thomas' newly completed *Summa Contra Gentiles* laid the foundation for a more stable philosophy in the service of theology.

Perhaps even more significantly, the newly proclaimed Feast of Corpus Christi and the supernatural beauty of its liturgy served to unite the Christian world in an expression of love and solidarity.

Thomas worked on in the somber stillness that settled on Orvieto after the pope's sudden departure and death. Before his exile, Urban IV had requested that Thomas write a commentary on the Gospels of Matthew, Mark, Luke, and John—and Thomas now immersed himself in that task.

To honor the memory of the great man who had been his friend, Thomas wrote his *Catena Aurea*, a "golden chain," linking the writings of the four evangelists with the most insightful spiritual commentaries extant. His work on that golden chain was a consolation in the long days and months following Urban's death.

In the winter of 1266, the clash of armor rang across a ridge between two rivers that lay just three days' walk from the quiet of San Domenico. On the fields of Benevento, Manfred Hohenstaufen faced Charles of Anjou. At first Manfred begged to negotiate, but Charles firmly refused. "I wish for nothing but battle, and that today I will either send you to hell or you shall send me to Paradise." Manfred resolved to die rather than to surrender, and his death came swiftly. After suffering a decisive defeat, he was fatally wounded at the hand of Charles himself.

His body was carried on the back of an ass and dumped into a pit at the foot of the bridge of Beneventum, where it was buried under a heap of stones cast upon it by his enemies.

Theodora d'Aquino's husband, Roger of San Severino, who had fought alongside the victorious king, was a witness to that historic final conflict. Charles of Anjou assumed control of Italy, but the war was not over. Young Conradin, the last of the Hohenstaufen line, was growing restless in Swabia, and gazing thoughtfully toward the turbulent Italian landscape.

Chapter Nine

THE LITTLE ONES

The confrontations between contending powers ceased temporarily in Italy as Charles of Anjou asserted his authority. Into the tentative calm that rested on the capital city of Rome, Thomas was sent by his order to establish a *studium*. It would be a small school of theology for the youngest Dominican brothers who were teenagers and young adults. His *socius*, Friar Reginald, and a small group of newly professed brothers accompanied him. They took up residence at the priory adjoining the Basilica of Santa Sabina on the Aventine Hill. There, Thomas began his first real experience of teaching at the level of the beginners, the "little ones of Christ," as he called them.

He lectured on Scripture, on the *Sentences*, and on the *Divine Names* by Pseudo-Dionysius—all the texts he had studied as a young scholar. But he soon realized that young men with no prior education, no matter how eager they may be, must first master the foundations of theology if they were to truly understand the richness of the faith and be ready to give an account of it.

It was a new kind of challenge for Thomas. All his life he had been hungry to learn, searching out answers, studying, plumbing the depths of the greatest minds, and sharing, debating, analyzing in the company of other scholars along the same path. Now he had to step back and look at what he knew in a different light. He had to discover how to guide young men who were just starting on the path of learning and who did not know how to traverse it.

These youthful minds were like plants that put out tendrils in all directions. There were so many distractions and confusions, not just among the young and the uneducated, but even among their learned mentors. Many of the texts available assumed too much prior knowledge, or presented the material in such a confused way that the truth was buried in an avalanche of verbiage.

"Like the riddle of the sphinx," Thomas reflected, "even in the life of the mind a man moves on four feet in the morning and on two feet only in the afternoon; he must crawl before he can walk or run." Thomas began to look back over his old commentaries, and to re-write them in language that was more accessible to beginners. He introduced to his students the custom of "disputations," a teaching tool popular at the leading universities. He knew that after reading a text and listening to lectures, a student has to have the opportunity to make the material his own. That was the goal of the disputations. Texts were publicly challenged and then given an accounting by the students themselves. It seemed to help, yet Thomas could see that it was not enough. How could he reach their young minds?

Thomas looked pensively out the window of the priory as he considered the question. A thriving orange grove spread over the grounds of Santa Sabina, The cool dark green of the leaves sheltering the bright orange fruit was a peaceful sight. Thomas knew that the grove on the hill was an inspiration to local planters.

Before Dominic de Guzman died, he planted orange seeds from Spain into its fertile soil. A single tree had sprouted and from its shoots, more trees were planted.

Seeing the multitude of trees that stood there now and their abundant fruit, Thomas recalled a parable once told by the greatest teacher of all to his disciples gathered on the shores of the Sea of Galilee. In that parable, a sower scattered seed upon the ground. Seed that fell onto the hard, unreceptive path was snatched away by birds, seed that fell into rocky soil took shallow root and shriveled in the scorching sun. Seed that fell among thorns sprouted but was choked out by the thorns. Only the seed that fell on good soil produced fruit, and it produced a hundredfold.

The soil that lay in the hearts of his students just needed to be cultivated so that the seed of truth could take root and flourish. His task was to make the soil rich.

Thomas turned from the window with new resolve. He found his *socius*, Friar Reginald, in the library copying manuscripts by hand. "Reginald, I have determined what must be done."

Reginald, unaware that anything had been amiss, looked up in surprise, "Did something need to be done?" Thomas' enthusiasm was visible as he exclaimed, "We must set to work at once!" Reginald set down his pen, gathered his papers, and followed Thomas out of the library.

Thomas described his new project. He would write a systematic presentation of theology, a *Summa Theologiae*, to guide the little ones of Christ. He would present the doctrines of the Catholic Faith to them, "as simply and concisely as possible in a way that would not bring weariness and confusion to their minds."

His *socius* understood and got ready at once to assist him, "It must be a systematic presentation of the whole science of theology," Thomas told Friar Reginald, "utilizing philosophy to explain, illustrate, and demonstrate what can be known about God. It should clarify what the mind can grasp on its own, and what it must draw from faith. It will address the moral life of man, making eminently clear the critical truth that love is the fundamental rule of life. To that end, it must present for the beginner the life of Christ and the life of grace he won. It must be comprehensive and, above all, Reginald, it must be clear."

Thomas wrote assiduously for the next two years, and he continued to lecture at his *studium*. His teaching was highlighted by his passion for the truth, and it was contagious. But at the end of that short time, he was called away from Rome. The order required his services as lector to the papal curia where Urban's successor, Clement IV, now presided. Another Friar was assigned to take his place as *lector primarius* at the *studium* in Rome. Thomas and Friar Reginald set out for the papal palace in Viterbo.

Forced to leave his "little ones of Christ" behind, Thomas took with him the work begun on their behalf. He was inspired to do this, a new apostolate that seemed to have fallen into his hands. In Viterbo, where Pope Clement IV was living, Thomas preached and offered spiritual sustenance to the pope and the curia, as well as to the Dominicans in his charge, but late into the night he dictated the theological masterpiece, his *Summa Theologiae*, to several secretaries at once. At the same time, he put the finishing touches on his *Summa Contra Gentiles*, and dictated the ongoing *Catena Aurea*. His work seemed to feed his spirit. He never tired, never flagged. He was conscientious in his writing by night, and in serving the newly chosen ruler of the Christian world by day.

Thomas had known the new pope, Clement IV years before as Sir Guy Foulques. In those days, he had been lightheartedly dubbed "Guy le Gros" by his friends in the court of Louis IX. He was a knight, lawyer, and councilor to the king of France. Thomas and Sir Foulques had met on occasion in the Great Hall of the king's palace in Paris, and at the priory on rue Saint-Jacques. At that time, Sir Foulques already had a distinguished reputation in law and diplomacy, as well as a charming young family. His beloved wife had died some years later, and when his daughters reached adulthood, he decided to leave the world behind to serve God as a priest.

The world, however, would not let go of him. He was appointed bishop and then cardinal. His piety and asceticism, combined with his intimate familiarity with matters of state, made him a natural for the role of pope. When the College of Cardinals chose him to succeed Urban IV, Guy Foulques begged with tears to be exempted, so well acquainted was he with the affairs of state. But the need was urgent and so, reluctantly, he acquiesced. Guy le Gros became His Holiness, Pope Clement IV.

He established his papal residency at Viterbo in the heart of Central Italy because it was deemed safer than Rome, his actual See. In Rome, the incendiary Ghibellines dominated once again. It was safer at Viterbo, but it was not serene. Italy quaked and Viterbo contended with Swabia for the epicenter. Thomas was able to offer spiritual guidance to the Holy Father, and the two were soon good friends. Clement IV valued Thomas' penetrating thought and his gentle heart. As the pope wrangled with the temporal powers of the world, he saw the enduring value of

Thomas' efforts to clarify for mankind the mind of the Church established by Christ, the Prince of Peace.

In their separate enterprises, in their distinctive ways, Thomas and Clement IV worked side by side. Encouraged and supported by the new pope, the Dominican Friar Moerbeke had just rendered Aristotle's account of the soul into Latin. This treatise, called the *De Anima*, was what Thomas was waiting for. He immediately went to work. He gleaned from Aristotle all he needed to understand and explain the nature of the human soul.

It was a timely topic for his work on the *Summa Theologiae*, too, and for the agitated world of academia. Making use of Aristotle's account of the universality of knowledge and the freedom of the will, Thomas saw how the soul of every individual must be immortal even though it clearly depends on the material of the body to function according to its nature. Aristotle's was a reasoned account that coincided perfectly with the article of Christian faith that maintains the resurrection of the body at the end of the world.

Scholars generally agreed that the soul had immaterial operations, such as reasoning, but were divided about whether or not the soul was merely the substantial form of the matter of each man, in which case it would cease to exist when the body dies, or whether the soul was itself substantially in every individual, having existence of its own that never corrupts.

This was the Gordian knot for contemporary thinkers. Through the careful reasoning of Aristotle set forth in the *De Anima*, Thomas had discovered an account of the unity of the individual soul, and a solution to the Averroist confusion that held the soul must be mortal, and so reasoning must be the result of participation in a universal soul shared by all human individuals.

Thomas' extraordinary powers of concentration served him well at Viterbo. Amid the political upheaval, he grappled with the academic and theological controversies of the day. He refined his philosophical proofs for the existence of God, and articulated the nature of law and the nature of grace. However, no one in Viterbo, or anywhere in Italy, could remain oblivious to the crisis on the horizon.

In the autumn of 1267, word reached Viterbo that the fifteen-year-old Conradin of Swabia, the last living Hohenstaufen, with his eighteen-year-old cousin, Frederick of Austria, had traversed the Brenner Pass through the Alps into Italy with an army of 3,500 men. Much to the chagrin of the Holy Father, Saracens in Italy were joining the German troops on his side of the border. He clenched his teeth, as many of the Italian towns in their path welcomed the Swabian prince with great fanfare. A new and untried tyranny held more appeal to the beleaguered people of Italy than the heavy-handed monarchy of Charles of Anjou.

Conradin gained confidence as he crossed northern Italy virtually unopposed. Pope Clement begged him to abandon his assault for the sake of his own safety, and for the sake of Italy, but he marched relentlessly forward. When the pope issued a decree of excommunication against him for his willful defiance, Conradin laughed. By spring, the army of Saracens and Germans had reached central Italy, and on Easter Sunday he paraded his army before the walls of Viterbo in a show of proud contempt. Looking on the parade from his palace, in the company of Thomas and many other friends, Clement was filled with foreboding. The pontiff shook his head sadly and murmured, "Like lambs led to the slaughter."

The struggles in the days that followed weighed heavily on the pope. Thomas saw his friend Clement grow increasingly discouraged as the tense situation escalated. Conradin and Frederick were young, and their opponent, King Charles, was unrelenting. The Angevin king had proved to be a harsh ruler, merciless toward anyone who opposed his will. He intended to impose order on a disorderly state, and would tolerate no contradiction. He did not abide by the terms of the treaty that brought him to the throne of Italy, and he did not apologize. Clement IV was at least in part responsible for installing Charles of Anjou as king of Sicily, yet he was powerless to control him. It was a bitter reflection.

In August of 1268, Charles' troops encountered the brash German youths leading their army through the heart of central Italy where only two decades before, Conradin's grandfather, Frederick II, had lived in grand estate. On the plains before the town of Tagliacozzo, cloven into the rock at the foot of the "Roman Alps," the two armies met.

Encouraged to find a surprisingly small defending army, the brash young Hohenstaufen ordered a head-on attack. Still naïve in the art of war, Conradin rejoiced—ever so briefly—over the easy rout of his enemy. Too late, he learned a merciless lesson in strategy. The troops he had beheld and defeated on the plains before him were only two-thirds of the enemy forces.

Hidden in a small valley nearby, Charles of Anjou waited with his finest soldiers. Within the hour, the invading army was ambushed by the king, and Conradin was easily and irrevocably vanquished. The two German princes fled through the rugged countryside toward the sea, escaping with nothing but their lives and their horses.

Rome, which had welcomed Conradin as the savior of Italy only eleven days previous, would not allow him to enter its gates as a fugitive. The two German princes were met before its walls by archers and pikemen in battle formation, lest they had formed military alliances in their flight from Tagliocozzo. Rejected by the capital city, Conradin and Frederick rode toward Naples hoping to board a ship that would carry them to safety. But word of their flight reached Giovanni Frangipane, an enthusiastic Guelf, who set out to capture them *en route*. Together with a handful of friends and dogs, he surrounded the fugitives in a wood only a few miles from the Gulf of Naples. The men met no resistance from the princes who by that time looked utterly dejected.

"What an unexpected treasure we have got! You may prove a useful bargaining tool, my young friends." Frangipane crowed as he led them along the coast to his castle prison in the *Torre di Astura*, a fortified tower that jutted out onto the Tyrrhenian Sea. But any schemes the captor might have had were soon thwarted when King Charles demanded that Frangipane turn the boys over to him. They must be tried as rebels and traitors, the king declared.

No one at the papal residence in Viterbo was surprised when word reached there a month later that the youths had been found guilty and sentenced to death. Conradin Hohenstaufen, it was reported, received the decision against him with calm dignity. He and his cousin Frederick had been playing chess while they waited to learn their fates. When told they were to be executed, Conradin merely lamented, "How my poor dear mother will grieve when she hears about this."

Clement IV was outraged by the decision. In the ensuing weeks, he begged Charles to be merciful to the youths, but to no avail. On October 29, 1268, Conradin tossed his glove into the crowd that gathered for his execution, as a final gesture of defiance. Both princes were beheaded on the public plaza in Naples, along with every accomplice who could be found.

Pope Clement IV died only a few weeks later, greatly troubled by the execution of Conradin and by the harsh Angevin regime that he had helped to put in place. Thomas grieved for his friend who had led the Church deftly through troubled times and had met the political powers of the world with benignity. His charitable purpose was frequently beaten down, but never broken. "Guy le Gros" had been a good friend, a prototype of disinterested leadership and of genuine charity.

After Clement's death, the Sacred College of Cardinals met in the papal palace at Viterbo to elect his successor. The conclave of fifteen prelates were hard pressed to agree upon a candidate who was both competent and willing to guide the Church through the prevailing political tangle. Their heated deliberations dragged on and on, without resolution.

When more than a year passed with no papal appointment imminent, the volatile Viterbians revolted. Led by the town nobles and burgesses, they stormed the audience hall where the Cardinals were gathered, approaching it from its two entrances, one through the elegantly arched loggia, and the other by the grand marble staircase at its entrance. The mob knew the floor plan of the palace well because they had completed its construction only the previous year. These were the benefactors, the artisans, and the laborers of that magnificent edifice. United in their annoyance with the long delay, they censured the surprised prelates in ungentle terms, and then locked the doors to the palace, setting guards at every outlet. The siege lasted for months while the weary cardinals continued to deliberate. The relentless people of Viterbo sustained them on sparse rations of bread and water until a decision could be reached.

Thomas was on his way back to the University of Paris before this revolt took place. Once more, he and his *socius,*

Friar Reginald, and a few other Dominican brothers made the journey over the Alps. Setting out in November, they paused occasionally at priories along the way to offer Mass, and to rest. It was a quiet journey, with Thomas often lost in thought.

How much suffering he had witnessed in recent years, and how clearly it manifested the existence of evil in the world and the need for mercy. Suffering seemed to be of various sorts, he mused. There is obviously the kind that conflicts with the natural desires; sickness, for example, conflicts with the desire to be healthy. And, of course, there is the suffering that contradicts the freedom of the will; no one likes to have his intentions thwarted. But without any doubt, suffering is of the worst kind when evil afflicts the innocent. Just thinking about it made Thomas shake his head and frown. Christ's agony must have been a torment indeed as He took upon Himself *all* suffering. How truly Aristotle spoke when he said that the greatest pity belongs to those people who suffer undeservedly. Of this last kind of suffering, Thomas had seen a great deal in his homeland.

"There is a kind of irony in the fact that suffering is caused by evil and discord," Thomas thought aloud, "yet it excites pity, which brings about unity." His companions looked up at Thomas in surprise; he had been silent so long.

"So there is," agreed Friar Reginald in an effort to answer him without interrupting his train of thought by pesky questions. Thomas continued, speaking now like a teacher. "When I pity a man who is in pain because of some conflict of will or desire, I enter into his suffering, which is the effect of love, and by that act our wills are united. Through mercy, I accept the other's suffering as my own." The men nodded, each one reflecting on his own experience of suffering and of mercy.

Thomas turned his gaze to the distant snow-capped mountains without seeing them; his mind was occupied with higher things. "How like God's mercy in its unity and self-sacrifice, and yet how deficient, is human pity." At last, Thomas looked at his companions and added reassuringly, "Still, we must do whatever lies within our abilities; God will make up for what is lacking."

His speech subsided as his thoughts turned to the tasks that lay before him. Complex issues under dispute at the University of Paris had to be settled, as well as critical questions to address in his writing. Truth is one, and it has the power to unite, he reflected; it is an instrument of mercy. Error is the father of discord. It leads the mind in diverse directions that inevitably give rise to conflict.

Discord persisted between the mendicants and their detractors at the University of Paris. And even more pernicious errors brewed among the faculty. Some highly influential professors asserted that the doctrines of faith *could* not be supported by reason. Others insisted that the doctrines of faith *should* not be supported by reason. Both were extremes that attacked truth at its core. Reason is the gateway to truth. To place an obstacle between the mind and its proper object can only serve to cripple the learners, the vulnerable, the little ones of Christ.

Thomas knew that the right use of reason, of philosophy in the service of theology, was not only possible, but crucial. His zeal moved his feet faster over the rocky alpine path toward Paris. The other friars quickened their pace to keep up.

When Thomas and his companions arrived at the University of Paris in January 1269, the faculty was once again on strike. But since that had nothing to do with him, Thomas assumed the Dominican chair for foreigners in the faculty of theology once more, and immediately began to teach. His first lectures were on the *De Anima*, presenting the philosophical and theological account of the human soul. Many of the fundamental errors being proposed at the University originated in a misunderstanding of Aristotle's account of the soul. He wanted to address those issues without delay.

A persistent anti-mendicant controversy at the university was gaining momentum at this time. William of Saint-Amour in exile was no less virulent than Master Saint-Amour had been in the seat of academic honor. Even while he lived in the far-off village of Saint-Amour, he had never ceased denouncing the mendicant religious. In his exile, he had written a third book condemning the mendicants and sent it to Clement IV as soon as that Holy Father assumed the papal throne. Meanwhile, he kept the furor alive at the University of Paris through continual correspondence with like-minded friends on the faculty.

These men, led by Gerard d'Abbeville, and the less vocal but equally hostile Nicholas of Lisieux, protested the right of mendicant orders to exist anywhere, but especially in academia. Their position gained support from a few bishops who resented the success of the Dominicans and Franciscans. They felt that the mendicants were encroaching upon their spiritual "territory," not to mention their sources of revenue.

During his lifetime, Clement IV had not acted on Saint-Amour's complaints because of the great good the mendicant orders accomplished. But Clement was dead and no one had yet replaced him as head of the Church. Saint-Amour could rest assured that there would be no official interference.

In the absence of papal opposition, Saint-Amour's good friends and allies on the faculty at the university took up the gauntlet and ran with it. Both were priests and theologians, not professed religious. They did not belong to any religious order, and they did not approve of any religious order. Gerard D'Abbeville, especially, felt strongly that religious orders denigrated the office of the secular priest. He wrote, lectured, and preached in opposition to the mendicants. His followers at the university, who were referred to as "*Geraldini*," joined the cause with a vengeance. He organized public forums attacking the Franciscan ideal of perfect poverty. He preached sermons denouncing the poverty of the religious orders and insisting that secular clergy, like himself, held an exclusive claim to the highest perfection of the spiritual life. In writing, he laid out his position that it is morally wrong for members of religious orders to study and to teach.

The mendicants united to meet the attack. Thomas' old friend and ally, Bonaventure, was no longer teaching but resided nearby at the Franciscan priory outside of Paris. He had recently been elected minister general of the entire Franciscan order. Thomas now occupied the Dominican chair for foreigners in the consortium of masters, and his former student and friend, Peter of Tarantaise, held the Dominican chair for France. Together they met the antagonists head on, defending the religious orders with the written word, in formal instruction, by public debate, and, above all, with their own irrefutable example.

Thomas published an explanation of the religious orders entitled *On the Perfection of the Spiritual Life*. In simple terms, he observed that according to the precepts of Christianity as set forth in the Scriptures, spiritual perfection resides in love of God above all things and love of neighbor as oneself. The religious orders, he explained, provide a means to achieve this state of perfection through the evangelical counsels of poverty, chastity, and obedience. Spiritual perfection could be attained in any state of life, of course, but the life of virtue fostered in the religious orders was most properly directed to that end. In that way, it was more perfect than the secular state, although, of course, he added, any individual religious man or woman may or may not be holy.

The *Geraldini* rejected this thesis, taking it as a personal affront. In retaliation, they published a collection of all the errors they could find in any of the writings of Thomas, hoping to discredit him. The debate continued in and out of the classrooms and lecture halls, even in the pulpits. Bonaventure joined the fray on behalf of the Franciscans with a second treatise on poverty, *Apologia Pauperum*. Thomas published a revised version of his treatise to answer the questions of his students and other faculty. At the conclusion of the tract, he admonished his antagonists to stop distressing the students and causing confusion in the classroom, but to publish their concerns "*so that intelligent persons may judge what is true and confute what is false by the authority of the Truth.*"

The disputed question was not resolved, however, and the *Geraldini* conceded nothing. But the concerted efforts against the mendicants ceased abruptly when in 1272, both William of Saint-Amour and Gerard d'Abbeville died within three months of each other. Without the vehemence of these two dynamic men, the controversy gradually faded away.

One afternoon after the worst of the turmoil had subsided, Thomas and a group of his students made a pilgrimage to the Basilica of Saint Denis north of Paris. The church was a paradigm of Gothic architecture at a site rich in Frankish-Christian history. It was built on land that once belonged to Saint Genevieve, whose prayers and diplomatic efforts had helped stem the onslaught of barbarians in the fifth century. It was splendidly decorated, but its greatest treasure for the pilgrims was the tomb that housed the relics of Saint Denis, a beloved bishop of Paris who had been martyred for his faith in the third century. All of France revered the saint. His name was on the lips of Frankish knights as they entered battle, shouting *"Montjoie Saint Denis,"* and in the hands of their standard bearers who carried the oriflamme flag of the Abbey Saint-Denis before them. Since the tenth century, the kings of France chose the basilica as their final resting place out of reverence for their national hero and patron, Saint Denis.

The students and their teacher were moved by the majesty of the building and the marvels God had worked in times past through his servants and saints. Refreshed and edified, this small group made their way back toward the university. They paused on a hill for a few moments to look out over the river, the spires, and the magnificent stonework of the city of Paris that stretched before them in all of its medieval splendor.

"How beautiful is the city of Paris!" exclaimed one of the students. Thomas smiled a little absently. His mind was absorbed with his work on the *Catena Aurea* at that moment, but he agreed, "Yes, indeed, it is beautiful."

"Please God that it would be yours," the admiring student suggested. Thomas looked at him, his dark eyes full of surprise. "What should I do with it?" he asked. The boy thought a moment, then he replied "Sell it to the king of France! And then build all the convents for the friar preachers."

Thomas laughed genially, and shook his head. "In truth, I would prefer to have at this moment the homilies of Chrysostom on Saint Matthew." He patted the young friar on the back and the amiable group continued their trek back into the city, united in the conviction that the homilies of Chrysostom were of course the greater treasure.

Chapter Ten

THE PIED PIPER OF PARIS

With the anti-mendicant furor subdued at last, religious orders were allowed to function in peace at the University of Paris. But a far more dangerous trend was emerging among the faculty. With consternation, Thomas and Bonaventure watched its rise and reach, which carried an almost impenetrable armor of intellectual pride. Young students were being led astray like the children of Hamelin. The persuasive piper was the Belgian Master of Arts, Siger of Brabant, who was little more than a youth himself. When Siger was in his twenties, he began to challenge the idea of a unified truth. He said that he had reached rational conclusions diametrically opposed to the teachings of Christianity. In the manner of Averroes, he declared that both the teachings of faith and his contradictory assertions could be "true," each in its own realm, but that his were the unassailable product of reason.

He had studied Aristotle through the distorted lens of Averroes and had fallen into the same errors. All human beings share a common intellect, he said. There is no original thought, nor any individual mind that thinks. Obviously, then, the human soul is not immortal, as Christianity claims, because it is finite and corruptible, inescapably bound to the body, which dies. The spiritual activity of the mind is undeniable, he admitted, but nothing spiritual can be bound to matter, so the reasoning activity of the mind is simply a participation in a universal "soul," shared by everyone. At death, the universal soul ceases to act on the individual. That is the end; there is no more. Thus speaks reason, he declared. Faith may claim otherwise.

Thomas recognized the influence of Averroes in Brabant's arguments. It was the logical consequence of a tainted understanding of the human soul. The notion that there can be two contradictory "truths," one for philosophy and an opposing one for theology, was illogical and easily dismissed. But the nature of the human soul was a more complex matter and the consequences of misconstruing it were grave. If the reasoning activity is not unique to each individual, as it seems to be, then the human soul is neither immaterial, nor immortal. It would follow that there is no life after death and, contrary to common experience, there is no free will by which we choose to act, there is no heaven, no hell, and Christ died in vain, for there can be no hope of eternal union with God.

Thomas knew that this is not so, and he had the philosophical map to the intellectual labyrinth in which Master Siger had lost his way. With anguish Thomas watched the power of Brabant's rhetoric take hold of impressionable young minds at the university. Brabant was a persuasive speaker. The students liked him and wanted to think he was right. Could someone who was so amiable and clever be wrong? The Bishop of Paris, Stephen Tempier, was also alarmed by the effect Brabant was having. He took note of the claims he made, and issued a condemnation of thirteen propositions that everyone at the university recognized as the philosophical and theological opinions of Siger of Brabant.

Siger was neither a philosopher nor a theologian, and Bishop Tempier begged him and his disciples in the faculty of arts to stop teaching about such matters. But Siger did not stop; he was confident in his arguments, and proud to be the bearer of light to a world he believed to be darkened by ignorance and religious bias. As his influence among the students at the University of Paris increased, the situation grew urgent. Thomas gave serious consideration to Master Siger's arguments and responded to them with a carefully crafted treatise, *On the Unity of the Intellect*.

Because of the great reverence that Master Brabant had for Aristotle, and the faint regard he had for Christianity, Thomas made no recourse to faith in this treatise; he drew exclusively on Aristotle's own words and works to demonstrate the immortality of the soul. In strictly philosophical terms, he argued that the immaterial activity of knowing arises from a power of the soul, called the "possible intellect," and as such, must be unique to each individual, not shared by all men, nor existing apart from the individual. In his account, the soul is the substantial form of the rational individual, but it is also the source of the immaterial operations of the intellect.

"From this careful examination of almost all the words of Aristotle concerning the human intellect," Thomas wrote in his conclusion, "it is clear that he was of the opinion that the human soul is the form of the body and that the possible intellect is a part, or power of that soul." Therein lay the solution to Brabant's quagmire. The pagan philosopher himself would have rejected Brabant's account of a universal "soul" because it did not account for the operations of reasoning. Master Siger had built his castle upon a foundation of sand.

"Master Thomas," a student stood up to ask a question at a *quodlibet*, or academic discussion session, which Thomas offered in one of the lecture rooms at the university, "is it not correct to say that shape makes a statue to be what it is? With a different shape, it would be a different statue. Is not the soul something like the shape of a statue? When the statue is melted down, its shape ceases to be."

"That is an excellent illustration," Master Thomas replied. It was an illustration Aristotle himself had considered. "The soul is indeed *something like* the shape of the statue. It is not however *exactly like* the shape of the statue. Shape, as you know from our study of Aristotle's *Categories*, is an accident inhering in a substance, entirely dependent on its subject for existence. The soul is much more—it makes the subject to be what it is in its essence. To extend your analogy, one might say that it vivifies the *statue*, bringing it to life and allowing it to do things that the shaped matter alone could never do. It is joined to the matter, but has powers that distinguish it from the matter."

A second student stood up. "Master Thomas, must one rely upon faith to hold that the human soul is immortal?" It was unclear whether the student issued his question as a challenge, or to offer an opportunity to explain his thesis.

"Aristotle, in his treatise on the soul, has demonstrated that the operations of knowing universal concepts, and of willing freely without constraint or pre-determination, are functions of the soul that do not rely upon matter, and are not subject to the limitations of matter," responded Thomas.

"Since these rational functions are separated from matter, their source must not be material. For, of course, an effect cannot be greater than its cause. The source of the rational functions is the soul. To answer your question, then, the soul of man can be proved by the use of reason alone to be immaterial, to be in fact, spiritual, and to be self-subsistent. As such, it does not rely upon the existence of the body for its own existence. It does not cease to be, when the body does."

Thomas' explanations were well received by many, but not by Master Siger who was too entrenched in his position to accept an alternative account. Condemned by his own bishop, and confuted by logic, but obdurate nonetheless, Master Siger remained at the University of Paris for several more years. For the sake of the young students, Thomas pleaded with him, not to "speak in corners, nor in the presence of boys who do not know how to judge about such difficult matters," but to put his ideas in writing instead so that all might know the foundations of his reasoning, and be better able to make a clear judgment about them.

"His honeyed words are like the music of a snake charmer, the students are entranced. But his music is, finally, tuneless," Friar Reginald expressed his opinion poetically.

"Yes," Thomas sighed, "it would be better if he set his thoughts in writing. Then perhaps even he would see how erroneous they are."

After years of damage done, and countless souls swayed by his rhetoric, Master Siger left Paris. He made his way across the Alps to the papal curia at Viterbo, hoping to convince the spiritual leaders there of his ideas. But something went badly awry. The students and faculty at Paris were horrified to learn, several months later, that Master Siger's secretary, who was known to be somewhat unstable, had brutally attacked his master before the gates of Viterbo, and stabbed him to death.

His end was violent and his legacy sadly tarnished by misguided reasoning, but his undeniable genius was immortalized in poetic verse by a renowned contemporary author, Dante Alighieri, whose own life was a tangle of political intrigue. In his trilogy, *The Divine Comedy*, Dante assigned a lofty place in the fourth heaven of Paradise to the eternal lights of "the twelve wise men of the past"—Thomas Aquinas, Albertus Magnus, Solomon, and Master Siger of Brabant, among others.

Friar Bonaventure, too, was assigned a high position in Dante's *Paradiso*, but it was not among that exclusive company of wise men. His "light" in the heavens was made beautiful, Dante wrote, by love.

Nevertheless, his practical wisdom proved invaluable to the beleaguered College of Cardinals at that time. Having heard of their captivity in the papal palace, and their unprecedented delay in selecting a new pope, Bonaventure traveled on foot the 840 miles from Paris to Viterbo. "If anyone can move those men, it will be Bonaventure," Friar Reginald said confidently. Thomas agreed.

Tired and dusty from his journey, but ever sanguine, the lean, olive-skinned Franciscan stood before the conclave in the great hall at Viterbo to offer his counsel.

"To begin with, let us call upon the first principle from whom all illumination descends as from the Father of Light. I refer to the Word of God, our dear Lord, Jesus Christ." Bonaventure's benevolent voice echoed in the hall. "Be true shepherds of the church of God, which he bought with his own blood. Do not allow your differences to weaken the sure foundation in which Our Lord Himself set the first stone when He declared, 'You are Peter, and upon this rock I will build my church.' Instead, open your hearts to the working of the Holy Spirit, the Author of truth and wisdom."

Every one of the men looked down, not meeting the holy man's gaze.

In a tone of genuine concern, Bonaventure continued, "I have come here out of love of the Church, and out of love for you—who are charged with its care—with a possible resolution to your quandary. At this time, there is active in the Church, a good man, Teobaldo Visconti, who I know to be filled with the love of Christ, zealous for the City of God, a man of true charity. He is not a cardinal. He is not a bishop, nor even a priest. He is an archdeacon and a secular member of the Order of Friars Minor, a 'little brother' who has pledged his life to God. In his voluntary poverty, God has made him rich in an understanding of the hearts of men, from the princes of the world to the littlest lambs."

He continued: "Visconti worked closely with our beloved pontiff of happy memory, Pope Gregory IX, in his difficult dealings with Emperor Frederick II. I personally encountered him later through his invaluable service to Pope Innocent IV at the first Council of Lyons.

"He is a man of unwavering conviction and, above all else, a true servant of God. My dear eminent fathers," Bonaventure spoke persuasively, "set aside what divides you and seek with purity of heart to secure that 'peace that surpasses all understanding,' for the sake of the kingdom of God."

Bonaventure's advice was readily taken by the abashed prelates, and within a few days the new pope was unanimously chosen. The secular Franciscan, Teobaldo Visconti, was to receive the papal crown. Visconti was in Jerusalem on a pilgrimage when word reached him. He was astounded, but obediently returned to Italy to take on the immense task. Accepting his appointment as a call from God, he was ordained to the priesthood. Then, without further delay, Teobaldi Visconti was consecrated as the long-awaited successor to the See of Peter, Pope Gregory X.

For more than three years, the Church had been without a pontiff. The Christian world rejoiced as Pope Gregory took up the shepherd's crook to lead the Church forward. He went to work immediately, calling a general council only four days into the papacy. It was to take place at Lyons, France, in two years' time. His hope was to tackle the pressing issues of Church reform, the place of the mendicant orders, and the division within the Church between East and West. Even before he took up residency in Rome, he began the groundwork for the council.

"Friar Bonaventure, you must play a vital role in this ecumenical council," he announced. "By the grace of God, may it pave the way to a lasting unity within the Body of Christ. We must likewise summon Friar Thomas d'Aquino, who understands well the issues that separate the East from the West. We have read his treatise on the matter. His presence will be invaluable."

The two Franciscans—the new pope, and the minister general—left Viterbo soon after Visconti received the papal mantel. As pope, Gregory took the entire curia back to Rome with him.

Bonaventure returned to Paris, and when he arrived at the university several months later, the minister general was alarmed by the extent of devastation he found there, wreaked almost single-handedly by Master Siger of Brabant. Promising thinkers had been led astray, and worse, souls of impressionable students were lost in the confusion. It seemed to Bonaventure and to his Franciscan spokesman at the university, John Pecham, that the study of Aristotle posed a grave danger. It must be prohibited, they firmly decided.

Like Bonaventure and John Pecham, Thomas was dismayed by the destructive effect the young and impetuous Master Siger had on students who came to the university unarmed against his subtle errors. But Thomas took a different approach to the problem—he believed the solution was not to ban the work of Aristotle but to present it more clearly than ever before, and without the filter of Averroes' misguided commentaries.

Since only a handful of reliable commentaries were extant, Thomas resolved to compose more, using better translations and more balanced argument. These would be faithful to the authentic intention of the philosopher. Without delay, he began writing commentaries on Aristotle's treatises on the soul, logic, physics, metaphysics, ethics, politics, and more. At the same time, he continued to lecture, to preach, and to work on his *Summa Theologiae*.

His secretaries were hard pressed to keep up with him; he rose before dawn to say Mass and to hear a second Mass, then he began his lectures for the day. Once lectures were completed, he ate his daily meal, oblivious to the food before him, and went to his cell to write. He wrote through most of the night, stopping only to pray the Divine Office and to rest for a few hours. To keep up his pace, he dictated to several secretaries at once on different topics, relying on his nearly infallible memory for sources and quotations that the secretaries later confirmed.

Occasionally he sat down exhausted and fell into a light sleep, but even that did not interrupt his flow of dictation. The secretaries kept writing while he slept, for he remained sitting upright and still speaking. Awake, asleep, or at prayer, Thomas' focus never flagged.

King Louis IX visited him frequently during these days, calling him out of his thoughts long enough to ask for counsel. The monarch valued the sympathetic hearing and sound advice Thomas always gave him. Despite all the work he was already doing, Thomas could be relied upon for a thoughtful response to any question the king brought him, written and dispatched without fail by the following morning.

The king respected Thomas' reluctance to leave the priory, but on one occasion His Highness urged Thomas to attend a banquet he was hosting at his royal palace on the *Ile de la Cité* in the center of Paris. Diplomats and royalty from all over Europe would be present to celebrate the completion of Sainte-Chapelle, a masterpiece of gothic architecture within the walls of the *Palais de la Cité*. King Louis had built the royal chapel to house the relics of the passion of Christ; it was a monument of gratitude to the King of Kings for the suffering he had endured out of love for his people. The consecration of that chapel would be an event of great moment to the king, and he wanted his Dominican friend to share it.

The day was indeed momentous. Men, women, and children lined the streets as their king, clad in the poor garments of a penitent, carried on a velvet cushion a crown of thorns that had once rested on the brow of the Savior of the world. He made his way solemnly through the cobblestone streets, and over the bridge that spanned the Seine. Sacred music issued from the newly consecrated chapel as its heavy doors opened to admit the royal pilgrim. An assemblage of bishops, priests, deacons, and altar boys joined him there. Beneath the blue-and-gold vault, they processed toward the altar, dwarfed on all sides by soaring panels of stained glass. Reverently, the king of France genuflected before the golden tabernacle, then laid the precious barbed circlet in its ornate reliquary of silver.

Throughout the rest of the day, people streamed into the royal chapel to view the crown of thorns in its magnificent setting, and to give grateful homage to their Lord and God who had once deigned to wear it.

Thomas had accepted the king's invitation to the banquet that followed out of friendship and obedience, although he would much rather have remained in the quiet of his cell at the priory. Seated in the great hall of the royal palace before a sumptuous table, surrounded by all the splendors of the court, Thomas noticed nothing. Inwardly, his mind continued to wrestle with the issues he was addressing in his work. His prior, seated beside him, was enjoying the novelty of the setting until he noticed Thomas lost in thought and using hand gestures to accompany the movements of his mind. Any faint hope that this would go unnoticed was dashed when Thomas pounded his fist on the table and exclaimed, "That's it! That will settle the Manichees! Reginald, get up and write!"

As the clattering dishes settled, silence fell on the room; all the nobility stared at the black-and-white-robed Dominican giant seated next to his flustered prior. Tugging at Thomas' cloak, his prior chided, "Master, you are now at the table of the king of France!" Thomas looked up and around the room, suddenly recollecting himself. Sheepishly, he looked to the king at the head of the long table and apologized, saying somewhat weakly, "I thought I was at my study."

Louis IX laughed aloud. Far from being perturbed, he understood the situation at once. Since Reginald was not among the guests at the banquet, he spoke to his own secretary. "Go over to Master Thomas," he directed him, "and take down his argument against the Manicheans lest it get away from him."

A similar state of abstraction often fell over Thomas when he was at prayer. Less than a week later, as he was offering Mass, the congregation became aware of long intervals of time in which nothing observable was happening. To those watching and waiting, time seemed to stand still with Friar Thomas at the altar. Finally, one of the brothers approached him, pulled on his *cappa*, and urged him to continue for the sake of the congregation. Thomas nodded his understanding as if in a dream. He went on, but his devotions absorbed his thoughts completely; the significance of the sacrifice he offered was overwhelming him. He consecrated the sacred host through streaming tears and repeated the prayers almost inaudibly, lingering long and lovingly over the words, "*Hoc est enim corpus meum ... mysterium fidei ... qui pro vobis et pro multis effundetur ...*" ("For this is my body ... the Mystery of Faith ... which will be given up for you and for many ...")

"Friar Thomas," one of the local men asked after Mass, "what happened in there? I thought we had lost you entirely once or twice during the canon," he laughed. "Are you well?"

Thomas flushed a little and said clumsily, "Oh, I am well. It was nothing. I am sorry." But the man noticed something—the friar's eyes seemed to shine.

Thomas' heart and mind were full to overflowing. All of his energy was directed to the unfolding of truth. He knew that reason brought a crucial light to truth, highlighting its contours, its richness, and its depth. To see and know by its light had the power to set the heart into flame, to evoke love and gratitude and hold one firmly on the path to God. How could that be anything but good?

Yet, at that same time, opposition was growing among some of his most respected peers at the university. The sudden awareness of it startled Thomas and grieved him deeply.

Chapter Eleven

A PARTING OF THE WAYS

"Perfect friendship is the friendship of men who are good and also alike in virtue; for these wish well alike to each other *qua* good, and they are good themselves." Friar Reginald considered Aristotle's account of friendship, encapsulated in those words, as he copied them out for Master Thomas' commentary on the ethics.

"Aristotle could have been describing Friar Bonaventure and Friar Thomas, when he wrote that," he thought, "were it not over a thousand years ago that he wrote it."

Thomas and Bonaventure were good friends, joined by a bond of charity that was almost visible. They had worked shoulder-to-shoulder on every controversy that confronted them. They were tireless compatriots in the City of God. But suddenly, they found themselves on opposite sides of a great divide. Bonaventure and his outspoken protégé, John Pecham, were wary of Thomas' project to clarify the teachings of Aristotle.

They insisted that because Aristotle was a pagan, his reasoning was suspect and could not shed a reliable light on the subtle truths of Christianity. Saint Augustine, the fourth-century Catholic bishop and theologian, on the other hand, was a trusted spiritual father, vibrant with the love of God, and unmatched in brilliance. Where philosophy was needed, they believed, his was the more reliable. Augustine alone could be trusted. Recent experience at the university verified that Aristotle could too easily lead people astray.

Their diverging points of view first came into open conflict when John Pecham incepted as master of theology. In his initial lecture before the entire consortium of masters, he condemned Thomas' well-known positions about the unity of the soul, and the creation of the world. Thomas believed that the world had a beginning in time, but that in its causality it was not limited by time. Brashly, young Pecham rejected Thomas' views and presented his own, which were directly opposite.

The eyes of many in the audience looked to Thomas expectantly, but he listened in silence, and asked no questions. Afterward, as Thomas walked along the rue Saint-Jacques back to the priory, he was surrounded by students who were outraged at the treatment he had received.

"Why didn't you object?" they asked. "You know he was attacking you!"

"Children," he answered, "it seems to me that one should be indulgent to a new master at his *vesperies*, lest he be embarrassed in the presence of all the masters. As far as my doctrine is concerned, I do not fear contradictions from any doctor, since with the help of God I have established it firmly on the authority of the saints and the arguments of truth." But the indignant students pointed out that the truth itself was under attack. Thomas reflected for a moment and conceded, "I will try to make up for it tomorrow."

On the following day, Pecham delivered his second address continuing the theme of the first. Thomas rose and said gently but firmly, "With all due respect, that opinion of yours cannot be maintained." Under the grateful gaze of his students and those of the faculty who comprehended the situation, Thomas calmly defended his view of the soul, of the creation of the world, and of philosophy as the handmaid of theology. These were the issues under attack. In a spirit of helpfulness, he laid out the problems inherent in the positions of the new Master Pecham.

His *socius*, Friar Reginald, was present at the lecture. He was delighted because, as he told the other friars that evening, "The truth became eminently clear when Thomas spoke. No other position was tenable, and Master Pecham could not but alter his language in the face of the irrefutable evidence presented."

Pecham did indeed alter his words to accommodate the situation that day, but he did not alter his opinions. After his inception, Master Pecham took every opportunity to contradict Thomas' work, ideas, and use of pagan philosophy.

Thomas was disappointed, not simply for his own sake but because he knew that the cause of truth would suffer. These good men feared Aristotle and revered Augustine, yet he believed the two thinkers were compatible, if rightly understood. The Augustinists, as Bonaventure, Pecham, and their likeminded followers came to be known, disapproved of Thomas' reliance on pagan philosophers and disagreed with many of the positions he held as a consequence. Against the Averroists, Thomas had borrowed the mind of Aristotle to show that the human soul is one and immortal. Although the Augustinists at Paris were repelled by the Averroist concept of a universally shared mind, they also disagreed with Thomas' account, which attributed to each individual a single soul.

The Augustinists maintained that every individual has many "substantial forms," not a single, unified soul. The multiplicity of forms, they thought, account for the various activities of a human being.

Turning once again to Aristotle's treatise on the soul, Thomas argued that there can be only one soul that actuates the matter of each individual—one "substantial form." The immaterial activities are evidence of its immortal nature, and its different kinds of activities are the result of powers of that one soul. The Augustinists found this doctrine distasteful and dangerous.

Even Bishop Stephen Tempier, wary in the aftermath of Siger's heterodoxy, sided with the Augustinists to oppose the use of Aristotle in the study of theology, and the conclusions that it led to. Bonaventure firmly resisted Thomas' approach to understanding matters of faith. The Franciscan master held that reason operated by a natural "light," while the things of God should be looked at with an infused, supernatural "light." Without that light, the mind goes astray, and cannot reach truth.

"Only faith can divide light from this darkness," he said. "This light the pagan philosophers did not have, and their arguments are worthless, leading to error."

Thomas held that reason may be applied even to matters of faith, if not to prove them, then to better understand them. The articles of faith, properly understood, he argued, are consistent with reason. He knew and attempted to show Bonaventure that Augustine himself would agree, but to no avail.

The whole unfortunate situation convinced Thomas more than ever of the importance of a solid grounding in philosophy. So many of these conflicts were the avoidable result of fundamental philosophical misunderstandings. Plainly, all truth was united and the reasoning of a pagan was as sound as that of a Christian in so far as it adhered to truth. He doubled his efforts to compose clear and reasonable commentaries on the works of

Aristotle. Whether or not his efforts would be met with universal approval was beyond his control. He could only perform his duties as he saw them. The rest was in the hands of God.

Saddened by the division among his friends and the disparagement he felt from some of them, Thomas turned his attention back to his work. He continued his simple regimen: to pray, to lecture, and to write. As provincial lector, he was responsible for providing a homily on Sundays. He prepared each sermon with great care, as he did all his writing, and his reputation for wisdom infused with holiness was growing. Wherever he offered Mass, the church was full. Articulate, soft-spoken, and sincere, he directed the hearts of his hearers to the highest ideas.

"Saint Paul wrote to the Corinthians, 'If a person possesses all the gifts of the Holy Spirit, but lacks charity, that person has no life.' Even if a dead body should be adorned with gold and precious jewels, it nevertheless remains dead. It is love, more than all other virtues, that gives life for this reason, namely, that charity attains God most, as its object and its end. For it matters not whether one has the grace of tongues, or the gift of faith, or any other gift; these do not bring life—without charity. The moral virtues, and the intellectual virtues are ordered toward God, but charity consists in union with God."

Thomas took solace from his own words. For although he knew Bonaventure disagreed with him, he recognized in his Franciscan friend the spirit of charity of which Saint Paul spoke, and Thomas, for his part, returned it gratefully.

In spring of 1272, Thomas presided over the inception of a new Dominican master of theology, and was free to return to Italy. He had done what he could in Paris on behalf of the mendicants. He had helped to quell the storm of Averroism, and he had demonstrated, at least to some, the need of sound philosophy at the service of theology. He was needed elsewhere, so his superiors requested that he return to Italy. Nothing was entirely settled in these years at the University of Paris, and it would be decades before his efforts came to fruition, but his work had taken root.

"There is still so much to be done," the rector of the university objected when Thomas told him he would be leaving. "Paris is the intellectual center of Europe, and you, Master d'Aquino, are its linchpin. Without fail, when the truth is challenged the faculty looks to you."

Thomas merely shook his head. At times like this, his shyness invariably surfaced. He was genuinely sorry to leave his friends behind, but he had been called away by the order; he had no choice. And in truth, the turbulence at the university was wearing. He had done all he could there. He would go where he was sent.

Chapter Twelve

THE SHADOW AROUND THE CORNER,
ALWAYS A PACE OR TWO AHEAD

Thomas and his *socius*, Reginald, set out across the Alps after Easter, in April, 1272, and by June 12 they were in Florence for the general chapter meeting of Dominicans. Their trek through the mountains had been relatively swift, and pleasantly uneventful, allowing time for quiet reflection and prayer. The grandeur of the Alpine spring directed the heart and mind to God.

When they arrived in Florence, Thomas and Reginald learned that the rector of the University of Paris, together with a number of the masters of arts there, had sent an official letter to the general chapter pleading that Thomas be sent back to them. But the order had other plans for Thomas. He was directed, instead, to establish a new theological studium for the Roman Province.

There were rumors that King Charles was going to rejuvenate the old *studium generale* in Naples. If true, it would be an ideal place and time for a Dominican school. Thomas, in the company of Reginald and a new student named Tolomeo of Lucca, traveled another three hundred miles from Florence to

Naples where his Dominican journey had first begun twenty-eight years before.

Along the way, the three companions stopped in Rome to visit Thomas' eldest sister, Theodora, and her distinguished husband. After his narrow escape from the siege at Capaccio, Count Roger of San Severino had fought beside King Charles on the Plains of Tagliacozzo to liberate Italy from the Hohenstaufen dynasty once and for all. Now he was the king's representative to the capital city of Italy.

Theodora and Thomas smiled to think how pleased their mother would have been with such a propitious connection. As they conversed, the other friars noticed a striking similarity in their gestures, and their lively dark eyes. Even their laughs were similar. Friar Reginald thought he had not seen Master Thomas look so relaxed in a very long time. Young Tolomeo thought he had never seen two people whose dignity of bearing was so evident, even when they were entirely at ease.

For Thomas, the company of this beloved sister was a welcome respite. A great deal had happened since their childhood days at Roccasecca, yet the years and the struggles seemed to draw them closer. Perhaps more frequent meetings would be possible now that Thomas was returning to Naples. The priory of San Domenico was only a few days' walk from San Severino.

From Rome, the three Dominicans made their way southward to the castle of an old friend, Cardinal Richard d'Annibaldi, whose nephew was also a Dominican and had been a student of Thomas' in Paris. But when they reached the Castle of Molara, they were dismayed to learn that the old cardinal had died. They prepared to leave the next day, but that evening both Thomas and Reginald developed high fevers and were confined to bed. After a few days, Thomas recovered, but the doctors did not think that Friar Reginald would survive.

Bitter would be the loss for Thomas if his *socius* were to die. Reginald had been his tireless secretary and a devoted friend ever since he first started work on the *Summa Contra Gentiles* twelve years earlier. Thomas began to pray fervently for Reginald's recovery. Remembering a relic he had brought from Rome, a tiny fragment of bone from the venerable body of Saint Agnes encased in a small gold reliquary, it occurred to him to give it to Reginald.

"Take this, my friend, and put your trust in the intercession of the good saint," he said. Reginald folded his hand feebly around the reliquary and let it rest on his breast. It seemed to bring him comfort, his taut face relaxed. Within a moment, his pulse steadied and the fever broke. He fell into a profound sleep. "Blessed be God in his angels ... and in his saints," murmured Thomas as he and Tolomeo slipped out of the room. The dumbfounded doctor followed close behind.

Thomas was ecstatic later in the day when Reginald awoke refreshed and sound and he declared to the smiling Reginald that from this day on they should celebrate the Feast of Saint Agnes as a solemnity, and he personally would host a dinner in honor of her, and of his good friend.

A few days later, the three men were on the Via Latina once more, heading south along the inland route. They stayed a few nights with Thomas' niece, Francesca, and her husband, Count Annibaldo, at their castle at Ceccano. Francesca's children were a lively troop of five boys, and Thomas thoroughly enjoyed their company. He spent every free moment with them in the castle yard, instructing them in the finer points of the game of *calcio* as his old steward, Mazzeo, had done with his family so many years before. He enjoyed their spirited conversation and their sense of wonder about animals and plants. It seemed to Thomas that the day for his departure came too soon.

From Ceccano they went on to see the Aquino family's castle at Roccasecca. It was empty and silent on the hilltop, but majestic nonetheless, and for Thomas, crowded with memories. He could have walked the path that led to the Abbey of Monte Cassino blindfolded without a misstep. Thomas took the other two friars there to visit the abbot, Bernard Ayglier, who had been a student of liberal arts with him at the monastery of San Demetrio.

That summer's journey stirred up feelings that at once delighted and pained Thomas. It seemed as if many people and places he had loved were lost. Yet the love they recalled was not lost, it was only out of reach for a time, a shadow just around the corner. In mid-September, the little Dominican band of three finally arrived at their destination, the priory of San Domenico in Naples.

Within only a few days of his arrival, Thomas was informed that his sister, Adalasia, had need of him. Her husband, Roger, Count of Aquila, had passed away unexpectedly a week earlier. Quickly, Thomas made his way north again, this time along the Via Appia to Adalasia's castle at Traetto, fifty miles away.

When he reached the castle and saw her with her four young children, his heart ached. The death of his tiny baby sister, Bella, came vividly back to him. He remembered the fear and mystery that had weighed on his childish heart, the pain in the eyes of those who were usually so sure, and the terrible, frightful loneliness. He grieved especially for the little ones. Death is bitter, there is no way in this life to escape its harshness, but he wanted the children to know that it is not the final victor.

At first, the children were timid around their uncle, who seemed to them as large and threatening as the giant black-and-white bear they had once seen in a traveling menagerie. When it stood on its powerful hind legs to look out of its cage it could not have been more massive than their great Uncle Tommaso. But their mother said he was to be trusted, and his eyes and voice were kind, so very kind. After only a day or two, they began to feel comfortable around him. They called him "*Zio Frate Tommaso*," Uncle Friar Thomas.

His nephew, who was the eldest of the four, spoke very little. But taciturnity was something that Thomas understood, and it did not unsettle him in the least. When they had at last formed a bond of friendship, Thomas gathered the children to himself, and spoke gently of their sorrow, "Do not be afraid, my little ones. Our Heavenly Father does not want us to fear. His love is so great, and so strong, that we have nothing to fear if we place our trust in Him. He wants us instead to have hope. Hope in Him, and in the day to come when you and your father will be reunited, as certainly you will one day be. Thanks be to God's great goodness. Until that fine day, we can do something for your father. You and I can pray for his soul, that it may rest serenely in the merciful heart of Jesus, just as he prays for you even now."

The children's consolation was not Thomas' only concern. Before his death, the count had appointed Thomas executor of his will. Thomas was responsible to dispose of the count's extraneous possessions, settle his unfinished business affairs, and ensure that these young children were provided for. When some of the practical transactions required royal licensing, Thomas walked fifteen miles inland to Capua to present his sister's case before King Charles of Anjou.

The king listened to Thomas and willingly agreed to all his proposals. He ordered his royal procurator to cooperate in whatever was necessary. Although Thomas and Charles had never met before, the formidable monarch admired the friar's intelligence and methodical, unassuming ways. From this time on, the king referred to him as "Our dear friend, Thomas of Aquino."

King Charles took the occasion of Thomas' visit as an opportunity to make his own request. Would Thomas be willing to accept students from the *Studium Generale* at Naples into his provincial school of theology? Confirming the rumors Thomas had previously heard, the king said he intended to restore the Neapolitan university to its former glory, and even improve upon it. He would require a competent master in theology and no one would be better suited to the task than Thomas of Aquino.

Thomas knew this would be a tremendous boon to the Order of Preachers, so he readily accepted. In gratitude, the king promised to pay an ounce of gold to the Dominicans at San Domenico for every month that Thomas was allowed to teach for him. Thomas smiled to himself, as he recalled the generous offering of gold his father had once made to the Benedictines for his education at Monte Cassino. How impressed he'd been as the child of five. Now he understood that the gift of knowledge, for which it was exchanged, was a treasure beyond price.

Thomas returned to Adalasia at Traetto to report his successful visit with the king. She was relieved of a great burden, and genuinely consoled by what her brother had done for her and her fatherless children. Thomas had ensured, with the king's approval, that Adalasia would have a place with their sister, Theodora, and her husband, Roger, who worked closely with the king. The children's education, too, would be in their charge. At last, Thomas returned to his duties at the priory in Naples, where the school year was already underway.

Thomas threw himself into his work wholeheartedly. In addition to studying, writing, and lecturing for the Dominicans and for the University of Naples, he held *quodlibet* sessions in which students were free to ask any question on any academic subject they wished. He had begun this practice in Paris and found it a helpful tool. The opportunity for students to discuss and ask questions about what they had heard in lectures or read in their texts was like the opportunity to savor a wine, to appreciate its subtleties and complexities, to make it their own.

In the wider community of Naples, Thomas' reputation continued to grow, and his sermons drew almost the entire population of the town, to even to his daily Masses. Oblivious to notoriety, he simply continued his routine, rising before dawn to confess his sins, to offer Mass, to attend a second Mass, to teach, to study, and to dictate the manuscripts he was writing. He kept several secretaries working at once, deep into the night, pausing only to pray.

With energy, he worked away at his commentaries and his *Summa Theologiae*. Illumined by reason and faith, he wrote about the passion and death of the Redeemer, and the sacraments that flowed from it. Tenderly he unfolded the mystery of the Sacrament of Love, the Holy Eucharist.

Early one morning, in the dark just before the dawn, Thomas brought his written account of the Eucharist to the chapel. Placing it on the altar, he knelt before the tabernacle and began to pray. The sacristan, Friar Dominic of Caserta, was attending to his duties earlier than usual that day, and instinctively retreated from sight when Thomas entered. He went on with his work as quietly and unobtrusively as possible until he became aware that

Friar Thomas did not move at all. Curious, but unwilling to disturb the master at prayer, he watched from the shadows.

In the stillness of the chapel, he saw that Thomas' face, upturned to the crucifix, was wet with tears that glistened in the candlelight. Then out of the stillness a voice from the crucifix spoke. "Truly," Friar Dominic told the prior later that morning, "I heard it plainly. It was a wonderful voice…full of…full of… I know not what. It was joyful and powerful and inexpressibly kind. It said, 'You have written well of me, Thomas. What reward will you have?' And in tones overflowing with love such as I have never heard before, Friar Thomas said, 'Only thyself, O Lord.'" The sacristan's own eyes glistened and his voice quavered as he reported the incident to his superior, who remained silent. Prior John of San Giuliano, who knew Thomas well, was not really amazed, but he was deeply moved.

Thomas became ever more abstracted in those days at Naples, lost in his own thoughts. He received many visitors but not always with perfect attention. His good friend and former student, the archbishop of Capua, brought with him one afternoon a prominent cardinal who had heard of Friar Thomas' reputation and wanted to meet him. Thomas was summoned from his cell but appeared not really to be aware of the visitors. He sat with them, nodding mechanically from time to time, his mind clearly elsewhere. After some uncomfortable moments together, Thomas blurted out unexpectedly, "Ah, now I have it!"

The cardinal was startled and indignant that Thomas seemed so indifferent to his eminence. The archbishop, who knew Thomas well, chuckled and told his companion not to take offense. "Thomas is frequently abstracted this way, no matter what company he is in." Then he gave a firm tug at Thomas' *cappa*.

As if waking from a dream, Thomas looked at his two visitors for the first time, displaying genuine surprise. He welcomed them warmly and apologized for his absentmindedness. "I am sorry," he said. "I thought I was still in my cell. A beautiful idea has just occurred to me for the work on which I am engaged at present. My pleasure in this simply burst forth in delight." The three men laughed. The rest of the visit was friendly enough, although the cardinal never forgot it, and the archbishop loved to tell about it. Soon it became a well-known anecdote in Naples.

For a year and a half, Thomas performed his duties with customary zeal as regent master of the Dominicans and of the University of Naples. He continued to study, pray, and write in every spare moment. He rarely left the priory, but would occasionally walk beyond the gardens into the picturesque countryside where Mount Vesuvius dominated the horizon, and the water of the harbor reflected the bright blue sky. His Dominican friends were amused to see people stop what they were doing and stare at his imposing stature and dignified features, softened with kindliness. For his part, Thomas was utterly unaware of their interest, but he always gave a genial greeting to any he noticed along the way. His thoughts were generally far away; there was so much to be done, so much to think about.

He had just begun writing a commentary on the Psalms of the Old Testament. The Psalms were as much a part of his memory as nursery rhymes are for many people. He could not neglect these, the fundamental furniture of his brain. The Book of Psalms, he said, was the key to all of Scripture; the entire life of Christ was foreshadowed in its lines and the whole of theology contained in its verses. He wanted to devote to them the profound consideration appropriate to a thing so richly layered with meaning. At the same time, he managed to make progress on his *Summa Theologiae* and on his other apostolate, the commentaries on the many works of Aristotle. He wrote and dictated at an extraordinary pace, driven by a sense of urgency that he could not really explain.

One day something ineffable reached out of the shadows and touched Thomas with a meaning so immense that nothing else mattered anymore. All his work came to a halt. There were no words, no image—there was nothing that could approach what he had seen. And nothing he could say or write any longer seemed important.

In the gray hours before sunrise, December 6, 1273, Thomas was offering a Mass for the Feast of Saint Nicholas, Friar Reginald of Piperno was serving. As often happened, Thomas became absorbed in meditation and tears began to roll down his cheeks. He moved slowly, and then he moved not at all. As he stood facing east, his eyes uplifted toward the host in his hands, he remained still and completely entranced for a very long time.

Friar Reginald remained patiently on his knees. He sensed that something was happening to Thomas, but he knew not what, so he waited and watched, and he prayed. Finally, Thomas finished the Mass, lost in an intense flood of emotion. Oblivious to everything else, he knelt long afterwards and then went back to his cell. He did not lecture as he was expected to that day, nor did he write, or even speak.

Friar Reginald followed him apprehensively. Thomas knelt in his cell all day. He spoke to no one. For days he remained wrapped in silence, oblivious to his surroundings, doing no work, eating nothing, sleeping rarely, but praying, just praying.

Finally, it was too much for Reginald. "Father," he begged, "why have you put aside such a great work which you began for the praise of God and the enlightenment of the world?"

"Reginald, I cannot," was all Thomas said.

Friar Reginald waited, and thought. Something was very wrong; always in the past, Thomas' work warmed and invigorated him. The master must work, Reginald thought, so he persisted. "Father, why are you no longer writing? Why are you always so remote and dazed?"

Thomas turned his gaze on Reginald at last, with a new expression in his eyes—and it took Reginald utterly by surprise. There was nothing of suffering or anguish, as Reginald had expected. What he saw looked to him unmistakably like joy; but not joy simply—joy pierced with intense longing. It was the look of one who has seen his heart's desire at last and found it more beautiful than he had ever imagined…and just beyond his reach.

"Reginald," Thomas sighed. "I cannot, because all that I have written seems like straw to me."

After a few weeks spent this way, Thomas said he would like to visit his sister, Theodora. He and Reginald set out for San Severino. After a slow and difficult journey, they arrived at the castle gates. The countess ran out eagerly to meet the friars when she saw them, but Thomas barely looked up; he said nothing. Theodora led the friars inside to rest. She asked Friar Reginald what was wrong with Thomas.

"He is completely out of his senses," she said, "and has scarcely spoken to me." Friar Reginald told her that he had been like this since the Feast of Saint Nicholas and had written nothing in all that time. Because the lady was so distressed, Friar Reginald tried once again to speak to Thomas.

When the two friars were alone, Reginald pleaded, "Why, Father, are you constantly dazed? And why have you given up your writing?" The anguish in his voice must have stirred something in Thomas' heart.

He replied, "Promise me, by the living God Almighty and by your loyalty to our order and by the love you bear me, that you will never reveal, as long as I live, what I shall tell you." He paused, groping for words. "All that I have written seems to me like straw, Reginald, compared to what has now been revealed to me."

"What is it, Father?" Reginald asked. But he received no answer.

When the Friars returned to Naples, Thomas became seriously ill and was confined to bed. A few weeks later, he received a summons from Pope Gregory X to attend the long-awaited council in Lyons. He resolved to go, despite the difficulty it would involve. He knew that the reunion of the Eastern church with Rome was a matter of grave concern, and close to Gregory's heart. He would not disappoint him. At the Holy Father's request, Thomas gathered up the treatise he had written to clarify the issues that divided the Church.

In February, he and Friar Reginald and a few other friars set out for Lyons. The council was scheduled to begin the first of May. As they walked, they were joined by others on the same route, also heading to the Council.

On the first day of their journey, Thomas, who was already very weak, struck his head against a large branch that hung low across the road that he had not seen, and was knocked to the ground. The others rushed to help him, "Are you hurt?" they asked.

"A little," he answered. But he stood up and, after a few moments, walked on with the rest, somewhat unsteadily.

Friar Reginald chattered amiably to distract his friend from the obvious pain. "This council will be a tremendous gift to the Church! There is so much good to be accomplished."

Thomas agreed.

"And I'm certain Friar Bonaventure and you will be made cardinals at this council!"

Thomas did not agree. "I can serve the order best as I am," he said firmly.

Encouraged by receiving any kind of response from the master, Friar Reginald indicated cheerfully that he was not so sure about that!

Thomas turned to his friend and spoke unequivocally, although kindly, as if to a child. "Reginald, you may be quite sure that I shall go on exactly as I am."

The party trudged on for several more hours, but finally Thomas became exhausted and asked to rest. They were not far from the castle at Maenza where his niece, Francesca, lived, so they all agreed to stop there. After a day or two, most of the others in the group continued on. Friar Reginald stayed behind with Thomas whose condition was not improving.

On the contrary, Thomas grew weaker daily, and could eat nothing. The physician seemed at a loss; but he urged Francesca. "Get him something to eat, anything he likes."

They asked Thomas what he thought he could eat. He could think of nothing, he wanted nothing. Reginald reminded him of some fresh herring they once had eaten in Paris. Thomas agreed that fresh herring was very good. Unfortunately, fresh herring was not easily gotten here, but the steward and the pantler were sent out to see what they could find. To their relief, the two men came upon a fishmonger on the road just outside the castle. He was selling sardines, but they ventured to ask if he might have any herring.

"No, sorry. Herring is difficult to obtain in these parts," he said. But he rummaged through his store of fish. "Well, look at that! Fresh herring! I didn't even know I had it!"

They paid the fishmonger handsomely and brought the fresh herring back to the countess for the sick man. There was such an abundance of it that everyone at the castle had some, even the many friars who had come to visit Thomas in his illness. Although Thomas did not really have an appetite, he took some gratefully. But he ate nothing more.

In the weeks that followed, many Franciscans, Dominicans, and Cistercians from the area came to the castle of Maenza to offer their comfort and prayers. To Francesca's children who watched from the parapet, they looked like ants moving in and out of the castle all day long. "*Zio Frate Tommaso* must be very popular!" one of the little boys observed.

"Oh, he is," his older, wiser brother assured him. "He's smarter than almost anyone. I bet no one knows the game of *calcio* so well as him. And he knows everything else, too. He's quite famous."

When at last Thomas realized that he would never recover, he asked to be taken to the nearby Abbey of Fossanova. "If the Lord is coming for me," he said with a weak smile, "I had better be found in a religious house than in a castle."

Francesca and a train of friends followed as he was carried by donkey to the abbey six miles away. When he reached the Cistercian cloister he touched the door frame and, quoting the Psalms, said softly, "This is my rest for ever and ever; here I will dwell for I have chosen it."

Some of Francesca's friends, who were following these events closely, asked one of the monks what Thomas was saying. "It is rather surprising," the Cistercian answered, "but he says he wants to remain in this cloister forever."

"Poor man," a woman cooed, "I don't suppose he realizes he is dying." Friar Reginald, who was inseparable from his sick friend, frowned at the group, and a respectful silence fell.

In subsequent days, as Thomas lay dying in their guesthouse, the monks cared for him, keeping him warm and as comfortable as possible. They read to him, prayed with him, and gleaned what they could of his wisdom. He protested that such good brothers had more important matters to tend to, and should not waste so much of their efforts on him. He said he would like to repay their kindness. He truly wanted to, but how could he? The men in attendance conferred with their superior about this and returned with a request. "Would you compose a commentary on the Song of Solomon for us, Father?"

There could not have been a more fitting task for this dying man than to unfold for others the answer to the question, "What is God?" as it lay within the passages of that text like a lightly hidden treasure. With his last strength, Thomas dictated a short treatise on this ancient testament of God's love that said in allegory what Saint John had later said plainly: "God is love." After a lifetime, Thomas knew it was so. His joy in his task was apparent, although it was taxing.

Finally, after a few weeks at the abbey it was clear that his end was imminent. In preparation for death, Thomas' made his last confession, giving his confessor, Friar Reginald, a general accounting of the sins of his entire life while the other monks remained respectfully outside the cell.

It was not long before Reginald emerged, his eyes streaming with tears. "The sins of a child of five," was all he said as he slipped past the waiting brothers. The monks assembled again in Thomas' room to chant the prayers for the dying. The old Cistercian Abbot, Theobold, carried into the room a beautiful ciborium of gold. Reverently he elevated the white host above it. This was the Eucharist, of which Thomas had written well, offered to him as viaticum for the journey of death. Thomas wept openly at the sight of the priceless treasure in the old abbot's hands. With shining eyes fixed on the sacred host, he uttered a prayer from the depths of his heart, "*I receive you, price of my soul's redemption, I receive you, viaticum of my pilgrimage, for love of whom I have studied, watched, labored; I have preached you, I have taught you; never have I said anything against you, and if I have done so it is through ignorance and I do not grow stubborn in my error; if I have taught ill on this sacrament or the others, I submit it to the judgment of the Holy Roman Church, in obedience to which I leave now this life.*"

On March 7, 1274, at the age of forty-nine years, Thomas passed into immortal life, a single, quiet soul face-to-face at last with the One Truth he loved and had lived to serve.

Afterword

"Friar Giacomo di Viterbo, Archbishop of Naples, often said to me that he believed, in accordance with the Faith and the Holy Spirit, that our Savior had sent, as doctors of truth to illuminate the world and the universal Church, first the apostle Paul, then Augustine, and finally in these latest days Friar Thomas, whom, he believed, no one would succeed till the end of the world."

(Testimony of Bartolommeo di Capua at the hearing of the case for the canonization of Saint Thomas, August 8, 1319.)

Standing before the Council of Lyons, seventy-four-year-old Albert the Great announced through his tears, "My son in Christ, Thomas of Aquino, the light of the Church, is dead." The silence that followed was charged with dismay. Everyone present made the sign of the cross and bowed his head. "Eternal rest, grant unto him, O Lord," someone intoned.

"And let perpetual light shine upon him," responded all of the men in a single voice.

"May his soul, and the souls of all the faithful departed," came the first voice again.

"Through the mercy of God, rest in his peace," answered the rest. They all made the sign of the cross again.

Then came an inevitable buzz of questions, comments, and expressions of grief.

"What a terrible loss!"

"How can it be? Last I had heard, he was on his way to the council."

"Such a young man!"

"And vital to the Church."

"Yet he was truly humble. They called him the Dumb Ox, but he was brilliant."

"I knew his brothers well, and his mother, may she rest in peace. His sisters will miss him sorely."

"How will we manage, even at this council?"

"Surely the man was a saint."

"He was indeed a great man."

The brown-clad minister general of the Franciscans sat silently amid the commotion with his head slightly bowed. His eyes, too, were, wet.

Over the next few months, Thomas' final resting place at the Abbey of Fossanova became a site of pilgrimage. Hundreds came to venerate the mortal remains and the memory of a man whose brilliance was unsurpassed, except by his charity. Called the Dumb Ox, humility had been the guardian of his intellect, and love the driving force. The people of Italy who knew him, or knew about him, did not wait for the Church to declare him a saint.

The rector, the procurators, and the masters on the faculty of arts at the University of Paris immediately claimed him as their own. They requested that his body rest in state at "the noblest of all university cities," they said, "where his youth was nourished, fostered, and educated, and where he had given the inexpressible benefit of his teaching." Their request could not be granted but the philosophical manuscripts that Thomas had begun during his tenure were accorded to the university by the Dominican order.

Although many people grasped that a great man had just slipped away, the tumultuous world of thinkers was still struggling to determine what was great, what was good, and what was to be shunned. In Paris, heterodoxy continued to plague the halls of the university. Pope John XXI asked the Bishop of Paris, Stephen Tempier, to compile a list of objectionable opinions being taught there. He asked for written evidence of those opinions and the supporting arguments.

In his zeal to purge the university of unorthodoxy, Bishop Tempier complied with the pope's request, but only in part. Within a month, he gathered a haphazard list of 219 theses that he considered suspect. Those of Siger of Brabant and his neo-Averroist contemporaries were on the long and varied list, along with some ideas derived from Aristotelian philosophy that were generally attributed to Thomas Aquinas. The Augustinist Bishop Tempier did not supply the evidence or the arguments, and without consulting the Holy Father, he condemned these opinions publicly as heresy.

John Pecham, when he became the archbishop of Canterbury, followed the example of his immediate predecessor, the Augustinist archbishop Robert Kilwardby, and condemned the teachings of Aquinas at Oxford. For fifty years after the death of Aquinas, there was confusion and undue hostility between his admirers and his detractors as a consequence of the condemnations at Paris and Oxford.

Much of medieval academia was not impressed by the condemnations, however. The Dominicans, for their part, threatened with expulsion any in their order who dared contradict or question the veracity of the teachings of Thomas Aquinas.

In 1316, Pope John XXII ascended the papal throne. Having been a student of philosophy, theology, and law, he had great respect for the work and life of Aquinas. As pope, he initiated an investigation into the possibility of an official declaration of sainthood for the Dominican master. It took twelve years of testimony and research, including interviews with Thomas' family and friends, and anyone living who had direct or indirect knowledge of him.

On the night before the canonization of Thomas D'Aquino on July 7, 1328, Pope John XXII proclaimed to the world that Thomas of Aquino had "enlightened the Church more than all the other doctors. By the use of his works, a man could profit more in one year than if he studied the doctrine of others for his whole life." For his sanctity, his fidelity to truth, his life of virtue, and his purity of doctrine, Thomas D'Aquino was proclaimed worthy of imitation, and of sainthood.

Throughout subsequent ages, the teaching of Aquinas has been upheld by the Roman Catholic Church as the paradigm of reconciled faith and reason. Pope Leo XIII, in the nineteenth century, declared that "Amongst the Scholastic Doctors, the Prince and Master of all, Thomas Aquinas, shines with incomparable splendor. Enriched with all Divine and human sciences, justly compared to the sun, he reanimates the earth by the bright rays of his virtues, while filling it with the splendor of his doctrine. Distinguishing accurately between reason and faith, he unites them in the bonds of perfect concord, while preserving the rights and maintaining the dignity of each." And, he added, "we cannot wonder at the immense enthusiasm of former ages for the writings of the Angelic Doctor."

More recently, Pope Saint John Paul II reiterated the significance of the work of Thomas Aquinas. "Saint Thomas is an authentic model for all who seek truth. In his thinking, the demands of reason and the power of faith found the most elevated synthesis ever attained by human thought, for he could defend the radical newness introduced by Revelation without ever demeaning the venture proper to reason."

At one time, nearly every institution of higher learning, whether Catholic or secular, built its scholastic edifice upon the philosophical foundation established by Thomas Aquinas. Even in this age of skepticism, his work has not been entirely neglected because it brings clarity to the questions that naturally occur in any age, in any honest inquiry.

Through the lens of his mind, the eye of the intellect is opened to the certainty and beauty of truth even now. Although much has changed in the world since the time of Saint Thomas, the human heart beats as it always did, and what makes it, moves it, and gives it hope is the same. Truth, beauty, and goodness remain the perennial path of hope, and along that path Saint Thomas still shines his light.

Notes on Sources

The beauty of biographical fiction, from the viewpoint of the author, is that the story has already been written in time, and found to be good. The challenge is not to come up with a new story, but to piece together an already-good story and present it in a credible way. To that end, it was never necessary to deviate much from the essential facts in this presentation of the life of Thomas Aquinas. The sympathetic characters were genuinely noble, the "plot" was rich and wonderful, the historical emperor, Frederick II, provided all the shock and horror necessary for an effective "foil."

Chronologically everything is accurate to the best of my knowledge. The challenge was to determine the order of events and where the central characters fit in, while supplying a context for the many authentic stories that have survived since the thirteenth century. In a story in which the central figure is as well known and revered as Saint Thomas Aquinas, it seemed unwise to try to embellish his character. His own words and deeds in this book are predominately as reported in the earliest accounts of his life. Much of it comes from the sworn testimony of friends and relatives acquired in the meticulous process to determine his eligibility for canonization. Some comes from his written work, and some are extrapolated from his work by people wiser than myself. The words of the supporting characters, friends, and family are authentic in some places, such as the words of Reginald of Piperno on the walk to the Council of Lyons, or the words of Albert the Great about the impact his prodigy will have. Others are invented to supply a plausible context for the rest of the story. The character of the family servant, Mazzeo, for example, is fictional, but it is likely there was such a person in the service of the Aquino family. The conversations and events that are imaginary are not wildly so. They were as plausible as I could make them, given what is known in rough outline form about those places and people.

The research as to when Saint Thomas wrote what he did, and why he wrote it at that time, is presented most thoroughly by James A. Weisheipl, OP, in his book entitled, *Friar Thomas D'Aquino: His Life, Thought, and Work* (Doubleday, 1974). This was a tremendously helpful book; I recommend it to anyone who wants to better understand the genius of Thomas Aquinas. Other texts that present worthwhile insights into the historical Aquinas, and offer an account of his thought are *Saint Thomas Aquinas, The Person and His Work*, by Jean-Pierre Torrell, translated by Robert Royal (CUA Press, 1966); *St. Thomas Aquinas*, by Ralph McInerny (University of Notre Dame Press, 1982); and *St. Thomas Aquinas "The Dumb Ox"*, by G. K. Chesterton (Image Books, 1933). The Jacques Maritain Center at Notre Dame University offers a wealth of information online, and the Thomas Aquinas College website (*thomasaquinas.edu*) provides intelligent presentations and articles bearing on the thought of Aquinas. For access to the simple facts in the lives of many of the historical figures, *The Catholic Encyclopedia*, published online by New Advent, is a reliable resource.

Information about the political life of medieval Italy was largely gleaned from the work of Oscar Browning, *The Guelphs and the Ghibellines: A Short History of Mediaeval Italy from 1250-1409*, and from a two-volume set entitled *The History of*

Frederick the Second, by T. L. Kington. Both are offerings of The Classic Reprint Series newly republished by Forgotten Books.

A book like this requires research and an accumulation of facts to be sure, but the heart of the story is something more than simple history. It is the conviction that truth matters, that it can be known, and is worthy of contemplation, that its Author is also the Author of love and of human happiness. I am deeply indebted to the founders and faculty at Thomas Aquinas College, a Catholic liberal arts college in Southern California and my alma mater, for swimming against the cultural tide to offer an education that recognizes that faith and reason are indeed compatible. Its curriculum inspires confidence that truth is accessible and is found most excellently in the mind and heart of St. Thomas Aquinas.

—Margaret O'Reilly

About the Author

Margaret O'Reilly attended Thomas Aquinas College in Santa Paula, California. After graduating in 1984, she earned catechetical certification from Our Lady of Peace Pontifical Catechetical Institute in Beaverton, Oregon. She taught high school theology and Church history at St. Agnes High School in St. Paul, Minnesota. Mrs. O'Reilly and her husband have twelve children whom they teach at home. Her articles on theological and apologetic topics have appeared in Catholic publications including *Homiletic and Pastoral Review*, and *The Catholic Response*.

America's Forgotten Founding Father
A Novel Based on the Life of Filippo Mazzei
by Rosanne Welch

A. P. Giannini—The People's Banker
by Francesca Valente

Building Heaven's Ceiling
A Novel Based on the Life of Filippo Brunelleschi
by Joe Cline

Christopher Columbus: His Life and Discoveries
by Mario Di Giovanni

Fermi's Gifts
A Novel Based on the Life of Enrico Fermi
by Kate Fuglei

God's Messenger
The Astounding Achievements of Mother Cabrini
A Novel Based on the Life of Mother Frances X. Cabrini
by Nicole Gregory

Harvesting the American Dream
A Novel Based on the Life of Ernest Gallo
by Karen Richardson

Leonardo's Secret
A Novel Based on the Life of Leonardo da Vinci
by Peter David Myers

Marconi and His Muses
A Novel Based on the Life of Guglielmo Marconi
by Pamela Winfrey

Saving the Republic
A Novel Based on the Life of Marcus Cicero
by Eric D. Martin

Soldier, Diplomat, Archaeologist
A Novel Based on the Bold Life of Louis Palma di Cesnola
by Peg A. Lamphier

COMING IN 2018 FROM THE MENTORIS PROJECT

A Novel Based on the Life of Alessandro Volta
A Novel Based on the Life of Angelo Dundee
A Novel Based on the Life of Giuseppe Verdi
A Novel Based on the Life of Henry Mancini
A Novel Based on the Life of Maria Montessori
A Novel Based on the Life of Publius Cornelius Scipio
Fulfilling the Promise of California

FUTURE TITLES FROM THE MENTORIS PROJECT

A Novel Based on the Life of Amerigo Vespucci
A Novel Based on the Life of Andrea Palladio
A Novel Based on the Life of Antonin Scalia
A Novel Based on the Life of Antonio Meucci
A Novel Based on the Life of Buzzie Bavasi
A Novel Based on the Life of Cesare Becaria
A Novel Based on the Life of Federico Fellini
A Novel Based on the Life of Frank Capra
A Novel Based on the Life of Galileo Galilei
A Novel Based on the Life of Giovanni Andrea Doria
A Novel Based on the Life of Giovanni di Bicci de' Medici
A Novel Based on the Life of Giuseppe Garibaldi
A Novel Based on the Life of Guido Monaco
A Novel Based on the Life of Harry Warren
A Novel Based on the Life of John Cabot
A Novel Based on the Life of Judge John Sirica
A Novel Based on the Life of Leonard Covello
A Novel Based on the Life of Luca Pacioli
A Novel Based on the Life of Mario Andretti
A Novel Based on the Life of Mario Cuomo
A Novel Based on the Life of Niccolo Machiavelli
A Novel Based on the Life of Peter Rodino
A Novel Based on the Life of Pietro Belluschi
A Novel Based on the Life of Robert Barbera
A Novel Based on the Life of Saint Augustine of Hippo
A Novel Based on the Life of Saint Francis of Assisi
A Novel Based on the Life of Vince Lombardi

For more information on these titles and
The Mentoris Project, please visit
www.mentorisproject.org.

Made in the USA
Columbia, SC
10 August 2018